D1083592

DOCTOR SEROCOLD

BOOKS BY
HELEN ASHTON

DOCTOR SEROCOLD

A PAGE FROM HIS DAY-BOOK

BY HELEN ASHTON

1930

GARDEN CITY, N. Y.

DOUBLEDAY, DORAN

AND COMPANY, INC.

PRINTED AT THE *Country Life Press*, GARDEN CITY, N. Y., U. S. A.

TO
LESLEY FINDLATER

VISITS PAID
BY DOCTOR SEROCOLD
ON OCTOBER 18, 1929

2:30 a.m.—Dr. Gaunt, River View.

9:00 a.m.—Morning surgery.

10:30 a.m.—General Meredith, 6 Water Lane.

11:00 a.m.—Miss Purefoy, The Dial House, High Street.

12 noon.—Town Council; Medical Sub-Committee.

1:45 p.m.—Cottage Hospital: Operations.

4:00 p.m.—Mrs. Unwin, Coldharbour Farm.

5:15 p.m.—Lady Catterick, Carfax Hall.

6:00 p.m.—Evening surgery (missed).

9:00 p.m.—Mrs. W. Sinclair, Gayfere Cottage, Water Lane. (Bridge.)

11:45 p.m.—Mrs. Perkins, 15 Station Road.

PART I

I

DOCTOR SEROCOLD sat through the small
hours of the morning, watching an old man die.

The bedroom was large, austere, and shadowy,
papered with faded rosy garlands and furnished with
heavy mahogany and marble. In spite of the fire
which smouldered in the black iron arch of the grate,
the doctor felt the chill of an October night beginning to settle in his bones; an uncontrollable restless-
ness continually obliged him to recross his cramped
knees and stretch his stiffened arms. The change of
position only relieved his fidgeting for a moment or
two: then it came back again, spreading his fingers
away from each other and setting his crossed foot
twitching. The sensation had become familiar to him
through forty years of such helpless, ceremonial
vigil; to ease it he rose from his creaking wicker
chair and moved toward his patient, though there
was nothing to be done for the snoring, staring, paralyzed old man lying propped against his pillows in
the shadow of the bed curtains, trimmed after the
fashion of the 'eighties with looped cords and tassels
and bobbing ball fringe.

The dying man was Doctor Serocold's friend and partner, Richard Gaunt, who had been overtaken by a paralytic stroke two days earlier, and now was gasping away an existence that had been singularly modest, selfless, dedicated, and empty of regrets. He had been a man of many small generalizations and proverbs, no friend to professional novelties, accustomed to work by rule of thumb and partial to antiquated remedies; a rough-and-ready, prompt but inelegant surgeon, an uncannily clever but utterly unreasoning master of diagnosis; abrupt, shrewd, and time-saving in his youth, an amiable gossip in later life, loved and delighted in by the three generations he had served; aged finally into a frail, indomitable gnome with bent shoulders, a completely bald and wrinkled head, and a toddling walk. There was nothing now to show that he was conscious of what went on about him; the fixed stare of the half-closed eyes did not waver before the light as it approached them, the empty, idle hands were limp when Doctor Serocold lifted them, the heavy breathing was already becoming irregular. Doctor Serocold waited for a moment or two with his hand on the failing pulse at the wrist, and reflected, "Not much longer now."

He stared at the waxen, impassive countenance,

and said to himself, "As far as one can tell, it's the easiest way there is of dying. I remember his saying once that he hoped he'd go like this. Well, he's got what he wanted. Marvellous that he lasted so long! He never told me his exact age, but he must have been twelve or fifteen years older than I am. Amazing, the way he's kept at his work! Got to the stage where he couldn't stop, I suppose. Some old men are like that. Right up to last week he was still trotting round, paying visits to some of his old cronies. Of course he knew quite well that he was past anything serious. He'd let all his operating go, and we'd managed to stop the night work, after his bronchitis got too bad. But he was uncommonly jealous about his old patients . . . wouldn't let me or Miss Gordon touch one of them if he could help it. They all backed him up, too . . . wouldn't call in either of us until they were absolutely obliged. Couldn't blame them for it . . . he knew every one of them inside and out, like one of his own gloves. He'd a wonderful memory: he could tell you everything that's happened in this town in the last fifty years. I'm not so bad myself, but he could beat me every time. Of course, he was born and brought up here, and his father and grandfather before him. I'm an outsider; I've only been here forty years. . . . It doesn't seem

as long as that to-night. I can remember the day I
came as if it were yesterday . . . walking into the surgery downstairs, raw from hospital, frightened of
everything and everybody, and knowing next to
nothing about my work. I wondered whether he'd
keep me after he'd had twenty-four hours to find
me out. Well, he taught me most things I know.
. . . This was a jolly house in those days, with his
wife alive, and the two boys growing up, and everything a joke to him; a good place for a young man to
come to. They'd not been married long then. An
uncommonly happy couple they were, sort of thing
you don't see so much of nowadays. She was sweet,
so gentle and amusing and clever: they understood
each other perfectly. A little woman she was, quick
on her feet, and quick with her tongue: I remember
now, she had brown eyes. Haven't thought of that
for years. . . . But she died, and the boys grew up and
went away. All very well for me, that was: I got taken
into partnership on account of it, though I'd no
money to buy my share with. But it was hard on the
old man that neither of the boys would look at his
profession. He'd wanted a son to come after him. I
can understand the feeling now, better than I could
when I was a youngster. But Dick was mad on his
notion of going into the navy: you couldn't have

kept him off it. And the other one was always a roll-
ing stone. Don't know where they got their taste
for seeing the world. Must have been from her side
of the family. Gaunt never wanted to go ten miles
from home. So there he was, with his wife dead, and
Dick always at sea, and Timothy fooling about in
Australia, making a mess of one thing after another,
till he came back and got killed at Gallipoli. And his
brother was drowned at Jutland, and there was an
end of it. Gaunt had to make some sort of a son of
me, poor old fellow! Not much consolation in that.
Well, he did more for me than my own father." And
with a heavy sigh he continued to finger the impulse
of life that was already lapsing to extinction under
his hand. "I wonder if he knows what's happening
to him," he thought, as often before at such a peaceful deathbed. "But one can't tell. I've been watching this sort of thing all my professional life, and I
know no more about it than I did at the beginning.
People think that a doctor can't care very much
about death, and perhaps while one's young one goes
through an indifferent stage; but that's over when
you come to my time of life. Death's getting more
important to you then."

And standing, at sixty-five, in the tall, broad, and
heavy magnificence of his stature at the head of the

bed, he wondered absently what had been the exact significance of certain symptoms which he had observed lately in himself. A little pain under the ribs, a little dislike for food, once a little vomiting, was honestly all it came to as yet: he had said to himself, and said it again now, as he would have done to a nervous patient, "There's nothing very serious in what you've noticed. You want more careful feeding and less smoking and a holiday as soon as you can get one: and your dentist will have to see to your teeth. You're too old for cancer of the stomach by a good five years." Some such words had been repeated to him three days earlier, in what had seemed rather too cheerful a tone, by the surgeon he had consulted at his own old hospital in London: and he had shied at them like a layman. "A bit too reassuring, Phillips was," he said to himself. "I've been telling people that sort of stuff all my life, and keeping the truth for their relations. I know just how much these encouragements are worth. I shall have to wait for the report of the test meal and the X-ray photographs before I believe him. He promised he'd send them on as soon as he got them. The letter ought to turn up to-day." And he glanced at the black marble temple of the clock on the mantelpiece. It was three o'clock in the morning, the time when life and courage burn lowest, and most men die.

He forced himself back to think of the old man. The end was very close; already the mouth was beginning to gape and the intermittent snoring to subside into a prolonged rattle. He would only need to wait a few more minutes. "Then it will be over," he said to himself; for with all his church-going, which was devout and regular, he believed in nothing further. "A long life, and a hard one, and very little reward. . . . Yet he always seemed contented. He'd never expected anything better: he did his work, and that was all he cared about. I wonder if he's satisfied, or if he'd like to come back and take a second chance." There was no hope of an answer: already his experienced eyes detected the onset of the final change in the worn and ravaged features of the old man. The eyelids had ceased to flutter and were taking on the familiar stare; the jaw was dropping open. There was no further movement under his watchful fingers, between the bones of the wrist. He waited a moment longer, to make sure, and all his own past life rose up before him, as it may to a drowning man. "Am *I* satisfied?" he asked himself. "I shan't be so long after him." He laid down the useless hand and drew the sheet up over the old man's face.

He said to the woman standing on the other side of the bed, "It's all over, Mary, I'm afraid."

She was as calm as he, though these last expiring breaths would change many things in her life. The widow of Doctor Gaunt's elder son, the naval commander who had been drowned at the Battle of Jutland, she had come with her two children to keep house for her father-in-law after the loss of her husband and the death of his brother. For twelve years she had been a daughter in the house where Doctor Serocold was almost regarded as a son, and the gossip of the town had more than once tried to remarry this widow and widower. It had seemed obvious that Doctor Serocold should become, if not his partner's son-in-law, at any rate the stepfather of his grandchildren; but nothing had come of the gossip. Luke Serocold had not married Mary Gaunt, or rather she had not married him: for once, when a spiteful old woman, Lady Catterick, had been talking to each of them in turn, he had asked Mary bluntly what she wished him to do in the matter, and she had replied with brusque determination, "Let them chatter as much as they like. I haven't forgotten my husband, and you haven't forgotten your wife. This need make no difference to either of us." He had admired her and agreed with her and continued to preserve his memories, which were of someone very different.

He looked at Mary now across the shrouded corpse and thought, as always, how fine and hard her beauty was, not with the crumbling hardness of carved stone, but with the spring and temper of a steel blade. She had singularly deep and hollow eye-sockets, as if she had wept them to the bone; her eyes looked out of them like living things in prison. Her beautiful head and hands were wasted by some perpetual hunger; her thin body, under its cheap black dresses, moved with a forlorn grace that he had always found unequalled. She was a strange woman; he had never seen her tears and never understood her thoughts.

She did not weep now. She fixed her dry and sombre gaze upon the corpse and said absently, "I'm glad it didn't last longer. He'd have hated a lingering illness. He'd done his work."

It was a good epitaph; Doctor Serocold admitted that as he turned to follow her. "I suppose you couldn't have a better one," he thought, going after her down through the silent house. "I shall be lucky if people say as much of me." He realized, however, that his old friend's death had shaken him: he felt cold and lonely and wearied out, and Mary Gaunt's indifference chilled him. He accompanied her without speaking into one of the living rooms. She lit the gas and knelt down on the hearthrug to break up the embers of a smouldering fire: a slight flame sprang up, with little heat in it. She spread her fingers toward it, and he saw their edges transfigured by light. She did not speak, but remained motionless, looking into the fire. He glanced round the room, to which the small hours had lent a peculiar unfamiliarity, though he knew it as well as he knew his own bedroom: it had been Doctor Gaunt's consulting room for all the years of his professional life. The old man had become of late years untidy in his habits and impatient of interference: the uncertain light of a defective incandescent mantel wavered upon the cracked black leather couch and chairs, the crammed bookshelves, the writing table littered with a confusion of papers, the shelf of disused bottles and rack of broken test tubes above the stained sink in the corner, all gathering films of dust. Doctor Serocold put his hand on the table and took it away again; brushed his fingers together and said to himself, "I suppose it'll all get cleaned up now."

Somehow the idea depressed him. "He never would let her turn the place out," he reflected. "That was one of the things she used to complain about.

She'll be able to have a bonfire now, all right. I wonder if she'd let me take the books. He had a lot of stuff I should like, not all medical by any means. He was a great reader. Now she never opens a book." And absently watching the beautiful woman crouching over the fire, he reminded himself, "Of course you couldn't expect them to get on. She was too stiff and cold for him, thought him a silly old thing, I shouldn't wonder. She was always one to turn up her nose at people she didn't appreciate. School-mistressy. . . . I can't stand the type . . . never could. The old man was afraid of her, I believe. But he'd made up his mind to look after the grandchildren. That was why she stuck to him. She'd have put up with anything for the sake of giving the boys a better chance, and Dick left her pretty badly off. This was the only thing for her to do. I must say she's stuck to her job, though she always hated this house. She's complained about it to me often. Of course, it's an inconvenient, Victorian place, ugly enough and, I suppose, difficult to run. She's worn herself out trying to manage it with young servants, and doing half the work herself behind the scenes. A doctor's house is always a hard place, with meals at all hours, and people coming and going. But I dare say the trouble was deeper than that. She never thought of the place as her husband's home. She never knew him till years after he left it. She doesn't remember him and his brother running about as boys here. I'm the one to do that. She only thinks of this house as the place where she spent the first, worst years after she lost him. She'll never forget that, and she'll leave it now as soon as she can get rid of it. Well, she'll be able to afford to go somewhere else. She gets all old Gaunt's money, and I dare say she thinks she's earned it. And I shall have to give her a thousand pounds for Gaunt's share of the practice. Not that it's worth it nowadays: but we put that in our original deed of partnership. And the grammar school wants the house for extra boarders. They've had their eye on it for years. The head master told me so. Mary will go up to one of those new villas on Camp Hill, and save all her money for the boys' education. I will say for her she's a good mother. She'd work her fingers to the bone for them if it would do them good. I admit they're a credit to her. Of course they're getting on. Time goes so fast nowadays. I haven't seen that elder one for I don't know how long. Natural, I suppose, that she should want to let him follow his father's profession. But I wonder how she likes his being so much away from her? Last time I heard, he was due for another six months

on the China station. Seventeen, is he? Or eighteen?
And Timmy must be round about twelve. I remember he was the result of his father's last leave." And
he said to the woman kneeling by the fire, "I hope
we didn't wake the boy." For Timmy was asleep
upstairs, having been kept away from his preparatory
school by an attack of measles, from which he was
now recovered.

If he had thought to soften her reserve by speaking
of the child, he failed. Mary said indifferently, "Oh!
Timmy's all right. He's quite got over the whole
thing. Even that little cough is gone. He was able to
be out this morning for two hours. I shall take him
back to school on Monday."

He thought again, "She's an amazing woman. I
should have expected her to keep the child with her
a little longer, now that she's left all alone." And he
said, "You really needn't do that, Mary, until you
feel quite satisfied about him. I'll give you a certifi-
cate for the school authorities. They won't expect
him till he's perfectly fit again." He was fond of
children, and the fact that he had none of his own
made him inclined to spoil those of other people.
But Mary said bleakly that education was the important thing, and that Timmy had missed a month of
the previous term. She added, with unmaternal de-

tachment, "He's a frightfully lazy child. He always gets out of hand at home. He needs a man over him."

"He'll miss his grandfather," ventured Doctor Serocold unwisely. She made no answer, and he gave it up: stifling a yawn of exhaustion and deciding that he need not stay out of his bed any longer to console Mary. "She doesn't care about anyone or anything but these two children of hers," he said to himself. "Thank Heaven, I never married her." And looking once more at the slender body crouching over the flames, he wondered suddenly and fantastically how it would have felt to take her in his arms. "A bit more than I should care to manage," he decided; and said aloud, with another choked yawn cracking his jaws, "Well, it's too late to talk over plans now. I'll come round in the morning and see whether there's anything you want."

"Don't trouble if you're busy," said she, cold as ever. "There'll be things to settle later, of course, about the practice and so on. And we shall have to talk over the arrangements for the funeral, I suppose. But there's no hurry." She rose to her feet and gave him her cold, slender hand: it hardly seemed to him living. He hesitated a moment more, feeling that he needed comfort; but she had none to give him and, with a weary resignation, he said, "Well, you've got the nurse to help you. If I can't do anything for you, I'll be getting along home."

Mary let him out into a dumb, mysterious autumn morning, in which a light fog from the river veiled the stars. A mild, misty moon stood still in a wide halo behind the chimney pots, and the moisture dripped heavily from the cypresses along the drive. The doctor made his way across the gravel and down to the gate, in a circle of pale illumination from his electric torch, then turned uphill. It was not three hundred yards to his own door. The old-fashioned red surgery lamp on its wrought-iron standard was burning weakly in the fog; he stood under it to find his latchkey, and opened the door more by touch than by sight.

He lived alone, except for the old couple who looked after him. Purvis, his man who had outlived the position of groom, now did odd jobs about the house and surgery, cleaned the car, and sometimes drove it, rather unskilfully; Mrs. Purvis cooked and cleaned, mended the doctor's old clothes, and gave him disregarded advice about his food. His house was in the High Street, at a corner and at the end of a row; it was tall and narrow, and built of a dark red brick that was the colour of old blood. The rooms inside were narrow also and disproportionately tall; the

windows were overshadowed on the street aspect by
the opposite houses, and obscured on the ground floor
by half-blinds of brown wire gauze. After his wife's
death he had given up this floor to his surgery, his
dispensary, and his waiting room. He now entered
this room, which gave immediately upon the street,
passed between its empty benches, glanced into the
unlighted dispensary beyond, circling his torch
upon its gleaming bottles and ghostly, dripping tap,
found no message for him on the slate in the passage,
and went on heavily up the stairs. He had an uncomfortable sitting room and even more uncomfortable
bedroom on the first floor, and as he turned into the
latter he heard the Purvises snoring placidly above
him. The room was cold, and, because he would
never have the blinds drawn at night, the window
stood open upon darkness; by day he had a clear
view of open country. He looked out now from force
of habit, but the moon was down, and the darkness
pressed against the panes. He sighed with regretful
weariness as he went about the cold business of
undressing, got into bed, mechanically made his
mind into a blank as he had trained himself to do,
and almost immediately went to sleep.

II

H E   W O K E to a bright autumn day and to the unusual fact that Mrs. Purvis had not called him. His
portly, old-fashioned gold watch, lying with its chain
coiled round it in the red velvet case on the night
table, told him that it was already nearly eight; and
he was accustomed to observe a surgery hour at nine
for his poorer patients. He tugged impatiently at the
faded woolwork bell-pull above his head, and demanded of the sunshine on the wall what had become
of the old slut.

She appeared after some delay, a small, bright-
eyed, voluble, bent woman, with an anxious flush on
her cheek bones and an indignant, habitual tremor of
the head. She was thoroughly accustomed to his
ways, and when he demanded with some violence
why she had not waked him sooner, responded with
equal agitation that she had intended him to take
an extra hour. "And you up half the night with
poor Doctor Gaunt," she protested. "You'll be busy
enough all day to-day, I'll be bound! What's the use
of that Miss Gordon if she can't take the surgery for
once, with Miss Ellice in the dispensary, that knows

all their medicines by heart? You stay where you are, sir, and eat your breakfast. I've brought it up to you." She had a rattling, overloaded black tin tray wedged against the doorpost, and she was panting as much from the weight of this as from the steepness of the stairs. She imprisoned the doctor, without any regard for his protests against a meal he hated, by depositing the tray across his knees; and he was obliged to rearrange himself cautiously, giving all his attention to the stability of the full teapot and the sliding dishcover, while he knit his bushy eyebrows together and grumbled, "There are half a dozen people I must see myself to-day."

"Leave me to sort them out," commanded the old woman. "I know who matters and who doesn't quite as well as that Miss Gordon." She always gave his temporary assistant this title, and disapproved of her youth and sex intensely. "Will you be wanting Purvis to drive the car, sir?" she continued, picking up his boots and resting them on one hip as if she were preparing to stay and gossip.

"No," said the doctor crossly, pouring out his tea. "I've got nothing outside the town this morning, and I'll drive myself this afternoon." He wanted her to go away and not to begin asking him about his partner's death; but he felt sure that she would do just that, and she confirmed his fears at once by saying, "There's many people'll be sorry to hear about the old doctor. It's all over the town by this time. I knew what had happened as soon as I heard the bell."

Only then did he become conscious of a steady, tolling vibration, mixing itself with the mild autumn air that entered by his open window. It must have been going on for some minutes; he realized that his ear had been aware of it, though not his full attention. He raised his head to listen, and the old woman became silent and listened also. Not until the gentle sound had ceased did she murmur, "The place'll seem different again without him."

The country phrase entered his thoughts and rang forlornly there like an echo of the bell. "Different again . . . different again." . . . He had not realized before how much of his own life would die with the death of the old man who had directed and shared his work. He did not feel that he could bear to face the thought; and he said, rather sharply, "Shut that door and get on with your work, Mrs. Purvis. We're all late this morning."

He knew that she would not misunderstand his mood, and she did not take any offense. She obeyed him in silence and left him to a meal that he some-

how did not fancy, though the morning was bright
and the day promised to be fair. He had noticed his
own loss of appetite lately: it was all part of the
train of symptoms that had set him thinking about
his health. Sipping distastefully at Mrs. Purvis's
stewed Indian tea, and wondering irritably whether
the morning's post had brought him any letters or
whether she had simply forgotten to carry them up,
he told himself that the day's news ought to relieve
his anxiety. "Phillips couldn't feel anything in the
way of a lump," he reminded himself, turning restlessly under the weight of the tray. "He said my
teeth might have a good deal to do with it. And the
old woman's cooking is no help to a man with a weak
digestion like mine. I told him I'd always had trouble
with my stomach when I was overworked." He was
perfectly conscious of the similarity between these
excuses and the encouragements that he might prof-
fer to one of his own patients. His mind began to run
over past cases and compare them with his own, and
he had to pull himself together with grim determination. "Haven't time to lie in bed and frighten myself
this morning," he muttered.

He pushed the tray resolutely down to the foot of
the bed, got up and began to dress; but he shirked
his weekly weighing, glancing sideways at the ma-

chine and persuading himself that he could not spare the time. It was the first occasion, however, for years that he had broken his own rule in the matter. Shaving, and scraping the lather from his big, heavy cheeks, he did peer rather doubtfully into the round, old-fashioned mirror on its mahogany stand and fancy that the handsome, fleshy, ruddy face he saw there was a shade thinner, paler, and less firm than the reflection to which he was accustomed; but he turned the key on the idea with a precision that had become second nature to him when he was busy, and set himself to plan his daily round.

He thought, as he plied the razor, "Thank goodness, it won't be a very heavy day! There's not much sickness about with all the fine weather we've been having lately. I must just look up old General Meredith and see whether his heart's troubling him, and there's Miss Purefoy's message about her maid, and the town council at twelve; otherwise, nothing pressing. Operating afternoon at the Cottage Hospital, but I've only that one mastoid case myself, if it *is* a mastoid. Must allow time for that, if necessary. I'll telephone before I go out. Wonder what sort of a night she's had. I did promise to give that anæsthetic for Jevons afterward—a nuisance; still, it can't be avoided. When a man hasn't a partner you can't decently refuse to help him out. He said it was only a matter of opening up an empyæma. Hope he won't keep me too long. He's very neat and quick, I must say . . . doesn't waste his time in the theatre; but he's rather inclined to push in an extra case at the end without giving warning. That won't do to-day. I must run up to Emily Unwin's after we finish. I shall be half-way to Coldharbour, and I promised two days ago that I'd see her next time I was out her way. Wonder what's the matter with her. She's been looking seedy lately . . . bad colour, rather, and getting thin; but she's not one to call in a doctor till she's obliged. Grudges the money, for one thing, poor woman, though she ought to know I shouldn't hurry her. It wouldn't be the first time, either, if I did forget to book a visit to Coldharbour, and she knows it. I'll go there on my way to Carfax. I told Lady Catterick I couldn't be with her much before five. Hope Harry won't hide himself away anywhere. I can't get him to talk when his mother's about, and I want to know whether those dreams of his are getting better or worse. She's such a liar, you can't believe a thing she says. But I must go into the state of his nerves, if what I hear about him is true." And plotting and contriving, as usual, to fit eight hours' work into six, Doctor Serocold hoped again, and more fervently, that Doctor Jevons would not keep him hanging about the hospital longer than was necessary.

He had a great, if unconfessed, dislike for the slap-dash methods of this young man, who had appeared in the town five years earlier, planted himself down in the slums near the station, and proved an unexpectedly formidable rival to the old association of Gaunt and Serocold. They had perhaps become a little insufficient for the needs of the town, even though they had set up a young assistant since Doctor Gaunt had begun to find his work a burden. Two doctors had been all that the place would carry in the sleepy days before the war, but in the last few years it had begun to grow. There was quite a large suburb out across the river, on the smooth chalk escarpment which the older inhabitants called Gallows Down, from the circumstance of a highwayman having been hung in chains there at some legendary date. "To be seen from four counties," had declared Canon Smollett, the previous vicar of Saint Luke's, who had been something of an archæologist, and had been responsible for this and other legends. The town council, however, had recently and tactfully renamed the site Camp Hill, because of its nearness to the new R.A.F. flying ground. Doctor Jevons had plenty of patients in the jerry-built little red-and-white villas and bungalows on Camp Hill, where the bank clerks and small shopkeepers lived. He was becoming popular, too, among the younger generation in the town itself, though their parents had remained faithful to Doctor Gaunt as long as he could do his work, and to Doctor Serocold after him. Some of them had even taken kindly to the latest assistant, Jean Gordon, who had come down from Edinburgh in a hurry, to act as *locum* when an influenza epidemic attacked both Doctor Gaunt and the previous assistant together, and had stayed on from week to week through the spring and summer, filling up the gaps in the practice with unfailing tact, cheerfulness, and resource and gradually making a place for herself that Doctor Serocold had little wish to empty.

He thought wearily, "But I shall have to do something about her pretty soon now, I suppose. She'll want to know whether I mean to take another partner or not, now that Gaunt's dead. Wonder whether she's after the place herself. She must have made up her mind about it by this time. After all, she's been here nearly six months. She's had plenty of time to think it over. But she doesn't give herself away." He smiled a little grimly as he recalled the vision of her round, rosy, inscrutable Scotch countenance, and admitted,

"I do not know in the least what the young devil thinks of the job, or the place, or me." For he was somehow unable to think of her except in the way that he would have thought of a handsome, careless, efficient boy. "She's never said a word about her plans," he reminded himself. "I dare say she only came for a few months' experience of general practice and doesn't mean to stay here in any case. She was raw from Edinburgh when I got her, straight out of hospital; I'd never have put up with her if I could have got anyone else. I must say she's been a pretty good bargain. She's taken hold extraordinarily well. She knows my ways and I know hers. I could train her up into exactly what I want if I chose to take the trouble. But I'm not sure that I want to. Bringing a woman into the practice as a permanency would be a big experiment, and there'd be a lot of opposition in town. People would gossip and object, and I should lose a lot of patients by it. Hardly the time to take a risk like that, with Jevons sniffing round to pick up anyone he can get! I haven't the heart for the experiment. I'd better look for a man with a taste for surgery, and fifteen hundred or a couple of thousand to put into the practice. But where am I to find him? I'm right out of touch with London nowadays, and I'm too old and too set in my ways to fancy breaking in a stranger. Shall I chuck up the whole show and sell out to Jevons? He'd give me as much as anyone else would for the good will, and I should be saved the trouble of hunting up another man. After all, why am I going on? What am I slaving for? I've no one depending on me, and I could retire pretty comfortably on my savings, with what I should get if I sold the practice. I might just as well chuck the whole thing and have a little peace and rest while I can. There's no reason for me to work myself to death." The word itself, however, startled him; and screwing up his eyes again at his own freshly shaven, florid, tired and somehow not altogether usual reflection, he had a return of the misgiving which he had deliberately banished. "Is there really something serious the matter with me?" he asked himself. "Did I actually feel that pain the other day? Does it matter whether I go on working or don't go on working? Am I done for, anyhow?"

And as he carefully cleaned, stropped and put away the old-fashioned straight razor, the use of which he had never discontinued, he became conscious that some part of his mind had for the first time made the peculiar observation, "At any rate, with this kind it's easy enough to cut one's throat."

He did shiver then a little, in spite of the sun on

the wall, and experience a precise, anatomical recollection of a throat that he had been obliged to sew up in the previous week. He told himself, "That's what's put it into my head, of course. I'm out of sorts to-day." And the professional part of his mind began prescribing coolly for the terrified, instinctive subconsciousness beneath it. He thought, "Doctors and nurses always go on like this when they've anything the matter with them . . . rake up all the possible horrors. It comes of knowing too much. I might be a third-year student! No use giving way to such ideas. I shall have my hand shaking next. Gaunt's death must have upset me more than I realized. Better get down and do some work. That'll put all this nonsense out of my head. I'm getting to the time of life when a man starts worrying over reports of inquests in the papers. *Deceased had been in poor health for some time . . . was acutely depressed by his own symptoms . . . kept the drug by him to relieve them . . . took his own life in the belief that he was suffering from an incurable disease.* Don't I know how these things start? I've had enough to do with them in my time. I'm not going to end up as the subject of an inquest if I can help it."

He finished his dressing rapidly, filled his pockets with their usual impedimenta—out-of-date wooden

stethoscope in the right-hand coat pocket, bandana
handkerchief and electric torch in the left, ther-
mometer, fountain pen and notebook in the inside
breast pocket, his fat, old-fashioned gold hunter,
with the circling pulse hand, in its place at the end
of a fob hung with seals, his money and his keys
balancing each other against his hips. But when he
had disposed of them all he turned absent-minded
again, forgot the surgery patients, who must by this
time be sitting in rows on his hall benches, and found
himself by the window, looking over the little town.

His house was the last of a terrace that stood on
high ground, and beneath it a limestone cliff fell
away into hanging gardens, supported by cracked
walls, steep lanes turning into flights of steps, and
crazy groups of wooden houses sticking like barnacles
one below another, so that the chimneys of one
smoked into the windows of the next. The whole
hillside seemed to be slipping and sliding down to
the patched vestiges of the town wall and the empty
wallflower-tufted towers of the Barbican gate. Beyond it the river took a turn about the low hill
of Castle Mound, where the shell of a Norman keep
rose out of a clump of elms with the jackdaws wheeling above it, and slid away between a double line of
willows, turning golden in the autumn air. The

angle of the cliff hid a desolate region beyond, where the water meadows had given place to the gas works, and the goods yard, and the rows of slate-roofed cottages that had not been there ten years earlier. From his window Doctor Serocold only saw the brown roofs, the weather-boarded buff and gray gables, the crimsoned leaves of the grapevine that wreathed about his balcony, the elder bushes sprouting from the face of the cliff, and the poplars dropping their yellow leaves into the hidden gardens as he had seen them any time these forty years when October came round. The smoke of the familiar chimneys rose placidly into an air that smelt of bonfires already; the sun of those mellow days which the country people call Saint Luke's summer dwelt upon the cracked roof tiles until they glowed with a warmth of their own. Behind them rose the immense and open sweep of a chalk down, crowned by a ring of beeches. It had always been his habit in the morning to lift up his eyes to that pale hill, but to-day they went no farther than the houses of the town in their encircling wall.

He said to himself, "I've spent all my life here and done all my work here, and I suppose I shall die here when my time comes. I wonder how much use I've been. I started with a lot of grand ideas, but they seem to have slipped away from me. I've been down here forty years arguing with people and cursing them, and trying to teach them something, but they seem to me to go on in much the same lazy way that they always did. Half the time I'm just patching up the troubles they've caused by their own stupidity, and the other half of the time I'm groping in the dark . . . sending them to bed, telling them to starve and keep warm, hoping they'll develop something I can diagnose, or cure themselves. I fancied I knew something once, but I'm getting rusty nowadays and lazy and afraid of work. I'm a solitary, bad-tempered old blunderer who's past his job. Time I made way for someone younger." But then, as he leaned on the windowsill and continued to stare down at the golden trees and crowded houses, his mood changed, and he said, suddenly and savagely and aloud, "But I'm damned if I'll hand the thing over to Jevons."

The sound of his own voice startled him; he thought, "Have I got to talking to myself?" and then he thought of the old man whose deathbed he had attended and listened again for the dull reverberation of the bell that he had noticed earlier. It had ceased, however, and there was a chime ringing briskly from Saint Luke's Church. He puzzled over

it for a moment before he recollected that the day
was the eighteenth of October, the festival of the
saint whose name he bore, the patron of the church
and of his own profession. It was the day on which
he had been born. "Sixty-five," said he to himself,
disliking the sound of it. And feeling that the sunshine
was less golden than it had been in past Octobers he
turned from the window and went down the dark
and narrow stairs to begin his day's work. The
morning's letters were on the hall table, and he
looked through them with hands which were perhaps
a little inclined to fumble, but they consisted merely
of circulars and medical advertisements. There was
nothing from the hospital for him.

III

JEAN GORDON was sitting behind her desk
already, working through his surgery patients at a
great rate and remaining as cool and unruffled as
ever. He admitted to himself as he went by that there
was something satisfying about her neat, round,
cropped head of fair hair, her rosy, freckled, sensible
face, and the unwinking stare of her green kitten's

eyes. He had never seen her hurried, or anxious, or out of countenance, any more than he had ever seen her untidy or at a loss for an answer. She knew what she did know with a prompt exactitude that amazed him, and when her knowledge gave out she never wasted any time in pretending that her memory had failed her. He was always pleased and amused by the way she had of walking into his room, putting her back against the door behind her, and demanding with an innocent and shameless confidence in his power to advise her, "What do I do in a case like this?" He liked to lay down the law to her a little; she took it so politely, listening and calling him "Sir" at the end of every sentence with a boyish respect that tickled his fancy immensely. She was as sharp as a needle, he considered; and if she did think that she could manage most situations single-handed, he, for one, was not going to undeceive her. She would get plenty of hard knocks from life before she was through with it, and they would probably take her innocent self-confidence away from her, but he did not suppose that she would come to any real harm. She was not the kind to sit down on a sofa and cry when things went wrong with her, as girls used to do in his young days. She had deserved a chance and he was glad that he had been able to

give her one. "But that's a different matter," he
reminded himself, "from keeping her on for good."
Still, he found this morning that the sight of her
refreshed him. She was busy with a child on her
knees as he went through the waiting room where
she sat, but she did just look up at him over the
mother's shoulder with a demure twinkle that delighted him, and he went on with a spark of warm and
fatherly amusement burning somewhere in his heart.

There were only three patients from his own
particular list waiting on the benches at his end of
the room. Either Doctor Gordon or Mrs. Purvis
must have sorted them out from the rest. He would
have them in one by one to his own little consulting
room, a dark and sunless place whose window gave
upon a courtyard paved with mossy bricks and occupied by a contorted fig tree. It was long past bearing, and each autumn Doctor Serocold resolved to
uproot it, but somehow it had survived all threats.
He made the usual resolution mechanically as he
glanced out at it; then took his seat and rang the bell
for the first of his patients.

Usually he enjoyed his morning surgery hour, but
to-day he felt depressed and out of humour, and was
merely irritated by a violet-faced, dropsical old
woman who wheezed and panted interminably over

her tale of bronchitic and cardiac symptoms, and a distracted young mother unable to quiet a spoilt and rickety child. They each took more time than he could well spare them, and after they were gone he still had to do a long and complicated dressing for a man with a badly scalded foot. He had to get his dispenser in to help with it, and afterward he felt it his duty to go back with her into the dispensary and linger for a moment among the shelves of coloured bottles and racks of test tubes, with his elbow on the slopped counter, and to ask her how her mother was. For his Miss Ellice, with her rabbit mouth and her twitching eyes behind their gold-rimmed glasses, was the slave and support of a woman who little deserved so much devotion and would certainly, considered the doctor, best serve the community by drinking herself to death as rapidly as she chose. Miss Ellice, however, could not be expected to share this view, and for the last ten years her life had been a fluctuating, prolonged, and gradually failing struggle against her mother's deceptively obstinate determination to die in the way that she had chosen. "You can't keep them off it when they get to that stage," mused Doctor Serocold. "We're just prolonging a hopeless situation by packing the old woman off to the home again." For Miss Ellice had

recently been persuaded to send her mother into an
institution for a few weeks, and had fretted about it
ever since. She had persuaded herself that the old
woman was unhappy away from her, and had moped
about her work and pestered the doctor with inquiries
as to when the cure would be over. She stood drooping now in the drug-laden air of the dispensary,
fidgeting about with her wet measuring-glasses and
beakers, and mopping in a spiritless way at a spilt
pool of disinfectant, while she recited her account of a
visit she had paid to her mother on the previous
Sunday. The doctor usually pitied her, but on this
particular morning his own depression of spirit made
him find her devotion annoying. He thought, "Anyone but a fool would say that she and I are wasting
our time on the old hag. She'd be much better dead.
She's no use in the world and I don't believe even
her daughter can really be fond of her. It's all senti-
ment." He concluded grimly, "Doctors ought to be
allowed to do a little licensed murdering, upon occasion." The whole affair had unexpectedly become
as stale, sickly, and sour-smelling to him as the odours
of the dispensary; and he stopped his Miss Ellice's
whimperings with an abrupt lack of sympathy that
was most unusual on his part. It left her with her
weak eyes moist and her narrow mouth gaping as

she turned to answer an impatient knock at the sliding shutter of the surgery. Doctor Serocold went away with the idea that he had stamped on something wriggling, distasteful, and defenseless; he was ashamed of himself and did not enjoy the sensation.

He thought obscurely, "And I can't give her notice. She needs the job too badly. Nobody else would stand her inefficiency, but I shall have to put up with that sniffling and complaining for good. I can't turn her adrift as long as she keeps off really serious mistakes. I don't think she'd ever actually poison anyone, though she's terribly slow and untidy; but she drives me nearly frantic sometimes. Still, I shall have to stand that. Even when the old woman dies she'll have herself to keep." For he knew all her circumstances, just as he knew the life story of every other person in the little town. It was the fruit and burden of his forty years there that he had learned a thousand troubles besides his own; each memory was a link in the chain that might keep him at his work until he died in bearing it. He half-turned to go back and say something less impatient to his Miss Ellice, but she was already holding a measuring glass to the window and peering into it with her short-sighted eyes, and he remembered the time and went back into the surgery.

Jean Gordon had finished her work already. The last patient had shuffled out into the street and Purvis, the doctor's man, with his russet-apple face, bent shoulders, and bandy, horseman's legs, was sweeping out the dust of their feet across the door-step and whistling a little between the gaps in his broken teeth, as if he were in a stable. Jean was at the cupboard behind the door, reaching down her leather overcoat, and she grinned over her shoulder at Doctor Serocold and said, "Good morning, sir," like a schoolboy. She had taken off the long white linen coat that she wore when she was working and pitched it across the back of her chair; without it she stood revealed in the silk shirt and the leather breeches that she wore for her motor-cycling about the country lanes, and her fair head was already covered by an airman's helmet with dangling ear-flaps.

He thought, "She's more like a boy than a girl," and then he thought, "I wish she were my son, or my daughter." It was an unconscious dream that must have been in his mind for months. It, rose to the surface of his consciousness like a bubble and escaped in a bursting sigh; and he said cheerfully, "You haven't taken long over your end of the work, Doctor." It always amused him to address her so;

and his eyes dwelt upon her quick movements with pleasure, as she shrugged herself into her stiff overcoat and began to button it all the way up to her chin. "There wasn't much to do this morning," said she, in her cool, pleasant Scotch voice. "Just old chronics."

"Nothing that you couldn't manage," he agreed with so much placidity that she never guessed he was teasing her, and answered blithely, "Not a thing."

His eyes were so deep-set under their shaggy eyebrows that she missed the quizzical gleam in them; she had, he realized, very little sense of humour. He inquired, "Where are you off to now?" and listened approvingly to the string of names that she rattled off for her country round. "Ought to get through that by one—or two—if you don't break down," he decided, and allowed the hidden smile to rise as far as his lips when she declared scornfully of the breakdown that it was "not likely." "Better take a swab from all those kids with the doubtful throats at Valley Farm," he told her, and enjoyed the immediate and deferential change in her expression. It made him think of another thing that he wished to say to her, and as she fastened the helmet strap under her chin, picked up her gauntlets, and waited politely for him to dismiss her, he continued soberly,

"No doubt you've heard that Doctor Gaunt died at three o'clock this morning."

The serious, official, attentive look on her young face changed immediately into something much more uncertain. She had seen little of the old man, but it had been evident that she had respected and liked him; it was for Doctor Serocold himself, however, that the note of pity broke into her charming voice as she burst out, "Oh! I'm so sorry for you. It must be—it must be——" She failed to find any words for the regret that widened her green kitten's eyes with helpless anxiety to console; and she stood there stammering in a way that really touched him. If he had wanted to see her at a loss he could do it now: she was quite inadequate for the occasion, and somehow this feeling which she could not expound was more of a relief to him than any flow of sympathy. He stood looking at her as if he had never seen her before, and for the first time since he had left Richard Gaunt's deathbed he felt the tears pricking at his hot and weary eyelids. He did not know whether the girl saw them and he did not care; his emotion was healing, and he could thank her for it. Almost at once he was able to control it. He said, "This will make a good many changes."

Her unblinking eyes were fixed upon him in a

childlike fashion. Evidently she did not wish to lose any word of his or any change in his look, and he found himself unable to meet her innocent inquiry. "I can't talk about all that yet," he stammered, perplexed.

She seemed to understand his reluctance and hastened to spare him its definite expression. "Don't you worry about me, Doctor Serocold," she began quickly, "I can stay here just as long as you want me. I'm not in any hurry to make fresh plans."

He said what he had never meant to say at this juncture. Something about the green and childish eyes forced it out of him. "Do you want to stay here altogether?"

She withdrew at once as if he had frightened her, but perhaps it was only her native caution; her start and slight frown made him add hastily, "You needn't answer that. I don't know what's going to happen. Everything's uncertain. I might . . . I might retire." He said to himself, "What the devil's the matter with me to-day? Why did I tell the child that? I don't seem to know what I'm doing." He could not hope that she had missed it; he told himself that she never missed anything to her own advantage. The green eyes glanced at him as sharply as a knife, but the girl said nothing; and he was

astonished to find himself appealing to her with a
weak desire for reassurance. "I haven't felt too well
lately. I went up to London the other day to get a
specialist's opinion. I don't suppose there's anything
seriously wrong with me, but it makes my plans
uncertain."

He saw her doctor's look at once, cautious, intent,
and protective; there was, he fancied, something
maternal in it. "I thought you were looking tired,"
she admitted, frowning.

He did not like this confirmation of his own fears,
and wished she had not said as much. "If she's
noticed it, too," he said to himself anxiously, "then
there must be something up." But he could not help
being touched by the gentle concern in her voice.
"I expect I'm fussing," he said aloud, despising
himself for a sudden wish that he had to sit down
then and there and tell her about his trouble. It was
not an impulse that he could indulge at that hour
of the morning, with all his work waiting for him,
even if her professional opinion had been of any very
serious value. "I dare say I need a holiday," he repeated, as much for his own benefit as for hers.

"You've had a good deal to do lately," she agreed,
but her brow did not clear. The black depression
of his spirits made him fancy that she was preoccupied

by the personal aspect of his news. "Of course, she's thinking that it may make a good deal of difference to her," he decided perversely, refusing to admit that he was being unjust. "She's planning her next move, away from here." And he said, rather crossly for him, "Well, you'd better be getting along. It'll take you all your time to do your round."

She accepted her dismissal as promptly as a soldier, swinging round and tramping out into the sun. He stood where he was for a moment or two and heard the explosive noises of her departure. The dingy waiting room seemed quieter, darker, and colder after she had left it, though he was vexed with himself for thinking so. He said to himself, "She takes everything very easily. But then, she's young. . . ." That morning he himself felt old.

I V

HE HAD a visit or two to pay in the town and meant to do them on foot; he had an old-fashioned taste for walking, and the cobbled streets were in the main too steep, narrow, and twisted for him to gain much time by using the car. Before going out, however,

he rang up the Cottage Hospital, two miles outside
the town, and inquired about the progress of a patient whose name he had for the moment forgotten.
She was a young woman from London who had come
down a few weeks earlier to serve in the post office.
Doctor Serocold had seen her there once or twice,
when he went in to buy stamps or despatch a parcel;
and had resignedly crossed her off in his mind as a
pallid, unhealthy-looking creature who seemed to
have a permanent cold, kept cotton wool in her ears,
talked in a thick, monotonous voice as if the back of
her throat were full of adenoids, behaved as if she
were half deaf when she answered the telephone,
and would probably make work for him sooner or
later. Now she had justified his forebodings by developing an attack of ear trouble which had obliged
him to send her into the Cottage Hospital for observation.

He inquired how she was, and the small, bubbling,
distant voice of the matron replied, "Not at all well,
Doctor. Her temperature's gone up another half-
degree since you saw her last night, and she's having
a great deal of pain."

"Slept badly, did she?"

"Very little."

"No improvement from the poulticing?"

"No relief at all, sir."

"No discharge?"

"No discharge."

He stood drumming with his fingers on the ledge by the telephone when he had the answer to that, and thought, "Then I shall have to operate. It can't very well be anything but a mastoid. Trouble with this ear before . . . an old discharge that's stopped . . . two days' pain . . . rising temperature . . . tenderness behind the ear. I've been hedging over it about eight hours too long as it is. I shall have her with a brain abscess next. The truth is, I funk these major operations nowadays. I'm a physician really, not a surgeon. I always used to leave them to Gaunt, in the days when experience would have been some use to me, and now I can't manage them properly. It must be a couple of years since I had a mastoid to deal with, and I shall have Jevons looking on. Well, it can't be helped. At any rate, he gives a decent anæsthetic."

And he sighed, and said into the receiver, "You'd better get her ready for operation this afternoon at two."

He heard the small voice reply, "Very good, sir," and them came a mysterious crackle and a silence. He hung up the instrument and turned away, thinking, "I'm not really up to this. If I'm not pretty careful I shall make a mess of it. A nice end to my professional career, that would be. Just my luck to run into something difficult to-day of all days. Well, it can't be postponed."

He walked out of his own front door, which stood open all day long, glancing as he did so at the brass plate, from which years of polishing had almost obliterated Doctor Gaunt's name and his own. He thought, "I shall have to have that altered, now he's dead;" and then, more grimly, "Better wait a month or two. It may be two new names by then."

He turned to the left along the High Street. It ran north and south, and at that time of the morning the pavement on his own side was in shadow. A little way along it he passed the bow-fronted window of the chemist's shop at the top of Easter Street, which was like a coloured picture out of Caldecott's nursery rhymes. It was stocked with a collection of old-fashioned rubbish, hardly visible through the small, dusty panes; dried poppy-heads, fly-blown packets of sheep-dip, stone hot-water bottles, cards of rubber comforters and sample bottles of cheap scent, all muddled up together at the bottom of the window under a flagon of coloured water as large as a child. Through the open door Doctor Serocold

could see the rows of glass bottles with gilt labels,
the majolica conserve pots and the blue ointment jars
ranged above the nests of mahogany drawers. He
knew that half of them had been empty for years,
and he sighed as he reflected upon the difference between this antiquated pharmacy and the smart,
bustling new shop down by the station, the branch of
a big manufacturing concern.

He thought, "Old Thompson makes too many
mistakes nowadays; he's getting blind as well as
deaf, and his hands aren't particularly steady. He
goes fumbling about that shop of his, losing things
or knocking them over. Sooner or later he'll do something serious, unless he can be persuaded to retire.
You can't blame patients for leaving a man when he
gets to that stage." The words struck him rather
coldly after they had passed through his mind; he
said, "Speak for yourself," and shivered slightly.
"But the fellow's older than I am," he calculated,
and said to himself that Thompson's business had
been going downhill ever since the old man's wife
died. He was a widower without children, and had
lived by himself for years in rooms above the shop,
with a woman to come in and do for him. Mrs.
Thompson had been a stirring, sour-tongued, managing creature, and her inefficient husband had de-

pended on her for everything. She had been quite
a young woman when he married her, and had always
seemed likely to outlive him. She had died, however,
inside a week, during the influenza epidemic of
1919, when Doctor Serocold had lost some of his
oldest patients and friends. As he walked now past
the neat little fanlighted door of the chemist's shop,
where the boy was carelessly beating out the doormat
into the street, he remembered Mrs. Thompson
gasping out her final breaths against her pillows in
the stuffy, overheated bedroom above, and her distracted, useless little husband wringing his hands like
a woman, and sobbing, "Janey, Janey, I can't get
on without you." "A queer type of infection we had
that year," reflected the doctor. "The lungs were sodden with fluid: you could practically say that the
people were drowned." And then he thought, "No,
Thompson couldn't get on without her. . . ." He
sighed and folded his hands under his coattails, as
he walked along the street with his head bent, in a
fashion of his own. Some bereavements are quickly
forgotten; others are like the dividing of soul and
spirit—what remains is not the whole of a man. And
he spared a thought for a story of his own, but had
dismissed it again before he reached the forge, where
Evans the blacksmith and his young son, in their

leather aprons, were blowing up the small flames in a
heap of ashes, to shoe one of the big dray horses
from the brewery.

Two doors beyond, the doctor had occasion to step
down into the cobbler's cottage with its leafy grapevine, and hand in a pair of boots for soling. He always
took his to Meek, because the man was an old patient
of his, a legless cripple with a weak chest, who had
been smashed to pieces on the Somme, patched up
again at Roehampton, and taught a trade for which
he had never been intended in his old farmhand days.
He now sat day in, day out, in an underground shop,
behind a counter littered with scraps and ends of
leather, companioned by an immensely fat and glossy
tabby cat. The doctor tickled it gently behind the
ears as he inquired about Meek's symptoms. The
man was always cheerful enough, in spite of his circumstances; he seemed to take a pride in his work
and to find enough of it to keep him. His shop was a
club for that part of the town; there were usually
three or four men gossiping round his counter in
the evenings, and the women ran in there for their
news. Doctor Serocold knew that he would not have
to tell Meek about his partner's death. Early as it
was, the man would have heard the story two or three
times already. Sure enough, Meek peered up at him

with his broad white face and blinking, red-rimmed eyes, and muttered a condolence. "'E was a good man," pronounced Meek. "A good man, 'e was. Shan't get another like that in a 'urry. I mind the way 'e sewed up me 'and for me, time I dropped me 'atchet on it." He stretched out his dirty left hand, with the tattooed snake circling the wrist, and displayed a seamed scar across the grimy cushions of the palm. "Near lost me three fingers that time," said Meek, with pride in the reflection. "Eighteen I was, and careless-like." It might have been the only wound of his life. Doctor Serocold thought, "Yes, I remember. You were the tallest boy in the town, and you didn't seem to care what you did, or whom you fought. I never seem to see a young man like that nowadays. They've all turned meek, and mild, and polite, and complaining. You were a great big hulking creature, with a stupid, cheerful face: and you were going to marry that red-headed girl of Evans's. But she went off with that German commercial traveller and you went all to pieces over it. And the war came, and your people were glad enough to get you out of the way. One of the town heroes . . . I dare say you fancied you'd get a smack at the man who'd taken your girl, or someone like him; and they expected you back again in six months' time, with a

string of medals and stories. They didn't think you'd
come home like this."

Meek was cheerfully inspecting his boots, remarking, "Down at the side as usual, Doctor," and offering him the choice between two different samples
of sole leather in a voice that seemed perfectly
content. When he could not reach a third sample
he said, "Excuse me, Doctor: there, by yer 'and";
and shifted his legless trunk actively along the bench
to pick up a tool. The doctor said, "This shop's no
place for you, Meek. You never get any sun, and
you're below the level of the pavement. Can't you
find a better place now that you're paying your way?'

"Can't afford no 'igher rent," said Meek. "Might
'ave took that place of Mr. Collins's at the corner of
Whitsun Street. They tell me it's empty now. But
the rent comes a bit steep, an' Mother an' Dad, they
don't care for movin'." His parents lived in a couple
of rooms above the shop, but he was too heavy to
be carried up the stairs, and the corners were awkward for his crutches, so that, as Doctor Serocold
knew, he slept in the corner of the shop. "I must
alter that, if I can," reflected Doctor Serocold as he
stepped up into the sunshine. "I ought to have
done something about it earlier, but I didn't think
he'd pull through as he has done. He must be pretty

tough. I thought he'd die off in a year or two. Men are hard to kill." And he wondered if he could do anything with Collins the grocer about the rent of the shop in Whitsun Street. He was not very hopeful about that idea, however. Collins was not the man to be generous with money, unless it belonged to other people.

He was standing at the door of his shop in his white apron as Doctor Serocold went by, a fat, jolly, red-faced man with a false appearance of geniality that was denied by the close setting of his little pig's eyes and the straight line of his small, disapproving mouth. He was one of the richest men in the town, a pious person, and a great supporter of the new Wesleyan chapel, whose distorted stone Gothic confectionery had recently replaced the comfortable old red-brick building, with the classic pediment, the crude stained-glass windows, and the wide gallery, at whose dedication John Wesley himself had preached. Collins did not care particularly about that; but he did care to see his own name on the cornerstone of the new building, and had gone to much trouble and expense to place it there. He was very active in the affairs of the town, and was now mayor for the third time. Doctor Serocold, as medical officer of health, had had several struggles with him on the town council over the new water supply, the necessity for repairs to some of his house property, and the inspection of a notoriously dirty dairy belonging to one of his friends. On second thoughts, it was not really probable that Collins would knock a shilling or two off the rent of a shop he owned in order to oblige a tenant recommended by Doctor Serocold. "More likely do just the opposite," the doctor decided. "I shall have to get at him some other way." And he nodded rather distantly to the stout man's greeting and reflected that they would meet at noon, when the town council sat. "I can slip in a word then," he said to himself, "if I get the chance."

He passed the fish shop of Alfred Jenkins, another town councillor, where the hose was gushing over the marble slab and one of the Jenkins boys in a wet blue apron was arranging a pattern of gray soles and dark green lobsters round a block of ice. At the next corner young Morton, the butcher's handsome son, was standing in the sawdusted entrance of his father's shop, hacking a sheep's carcass to pieces between the doorposts. He grinned at the doctor, who had hooked him into the world by one leg, pulled out his teeth for him when he was small, sent him home on one occasion for playing in the street with a measles rash on his face, and sewn up his

foot for him the previous Christmas when he dropped
a chopper on it. The doctor nodded back, approving
the round, rosy face, the black hair shining with
suet, broad shoulders and roving eye, and thought,
"Yes, you're a fine lad. Your parents did pretty
well for you, taking it all round. It's a pity you didn't
choose a better mother for your children while you
were about it." Young Mrs. Morton had been a
teacher at the grammar school, and it had taken
some time to overcome her notion that she was de-
meaning herself by marrying a butcher. She was
a pretty, silly, London-bred girl, with fuzzy hair, a
pale face, and a thin, high, genteel way of talking;
narrow in the hips and round in the shoulders. She
had been married five years and had no children;
and recently Doctor Serocold had begun to treat her
for diabetic tendencies. She was sitting at the cash
desk of the shop as he went by, for she sometimes
gave a little reluctant help with the bookkeeping
when Morton & Son were short-handed. She did
not see the doctor, but he heard her fretfully screeching down the telephone, "Loin of Canterbury lamb,
about eight bones . . . two pounds best rump . . .
half English kidney . . . half of suet . . ." He felt
sorry for young Morton, who had to listen to that
voice all day, and was supposed to be realizing that

his marriage had been a mistake. He looked cheerful
enough, however, as he hacked away at his mutton
and whistled to himself: Doctor Serocold had been
told that the roving eye had already found consolation elsewhere. He turned down Church Hill, reflecting grimly that young Morton, as a father, was
not likely to be permanently wasted.

At the bottom of the hill the sun was already
shining through the great Perpendicular window
which closed the north transept of Saint Luke's
Church with a wall of glass. The fourteenth-century
clock on the tall tower with the stone lattices and
pinnacles marked three minutes to ten, and he
lingered on the hill for the mere childish pleasure of
watching the hour strike. He had done the same
thing any morning these forty years. There was a
drumming wooden figure in a black-and-white
uniform, with a comical red face, who beat the quarters, and there were a couple of knights on horseback
who rode a-tilt at each other at the half-hours: but
at the hour a pair of obese and gilded cherubs each
raised a hand, with a disproportionate amount of
effort, and struck weakly at the bell that hung between them, and a cock came out and raised its head
as if to crow. Doctor Serocold waited gravely until
the whole performance was over before he moved on.

with a faint smile on his face, either for the cherubs or for himself.

He passed the pawnbroker's and the circulating library, and the new tea shop, with its aggressive black-and-white, half-timbered gables, its jade-and-orange curtains, latticed windows full of lopsided, home-made cakes, and swinging sign of a ship in full sail, "The Bold Adventure." The strong, sweet smell of boiling jam came from the open door. "Blackberries," he decided; "the first I've smelt. I wish I could get Mrs. Purvis to make some." A young woman emerged lugging out a notice board with an inscription in uncertain old English lettering, and Doctor Serocold, who had kept his eye for a pretty face, took off his hat to her as she propped her board uncertainly against a blue tub with a bay tree in it, glanced at the neat blue window-boxes, still full of Michaelmas daisies, and walked on, thinking, "Those girls have chosen a good position. Half the trippers must go by on their way back to the High Street from the church. The hill's too steep for the chars-à-bancs, luckily, otherwise we should have the beastly things all round the churchyard. At least that's quiet. But it's a good pull up to the High Street again. I've noticed it myself lately. There's more fat in my heart muscle than there used

to be, I'm afraid. No wonder the trippers stop at the
tea shop, half-way up. The street's like the side of a
house, and the girls have got the window looking
very enticing. I never go by in the afternoon without
seeing the place full. They must be making quite a
good thing out of the business. But you can always
turn your money over if you go in for selling food.
It's a greedy world, luckily for tea-shop keepers,
and for me. Half my patients would dig their graves
with their teeth if they were left alone. I make a lot
of money out of over-eating." And with his sour
smile creasing his face into wrinkles he strolled on,
thinking, "I wish the two of them luck, I'm sure.
It must have taken some pluck to start in a strange
place as they did. But there are too many women in
this town nowadays. It was always crowded with
'em, and since the war it seems to me ten times
worse, especially as they all do things. I can't get
used to it. In my day they stopped at home and
kept quiet, and if some of them *were* a little odd,
well, it wasn't talked about."

His meditations had taken him down as far as
Saint Luke's Close. The church, a very large Perpendicular building, with a disproportionate number
of windows and an unsually tall spire, stood in the
bottom of a hollow, between the twin hills on which

the town was built. It was surrounded by a green graveyard, full of dilapidated altar-tombs, leaning stones carved with the heads of cherubs, and unnamed mounds sinking into the long herbage between the clipped yews. There had been no new graves for a long time, and there was an air of peaceful neglect about the place that suggested a village rather than a town. The close was shut in by the backs of a number of tumbledown cottages, with blocked windows and walls smothered in ivy: it was a silent corner, haunted by prowling cats, a couple of whom were now stretched together on a tombstone, industriously licking the sunshine from their paws. Doctor Serocold looked at the cats, which were both glossy, black, and very thin, and said to himself, "If this were the Middle Ages, they'd both be taken for witches, hanging about all day in the churchyard and thinking of bones."

V

HE TOOK the path, paved with obliterated tombstones, which led round to the south door, and as he walked past the second of the ivied cottages he thought, "England's full of queer people. In a country town like this you get 'em as queer as anywhere. I used to think the oddities all ended up in asylums, but upon my word I'm coming to think there are more of them outside the recognized institutions than in. I can remember a dozen who could have been locked up if they'd had any relatives to take the trouble, or any money to make them fair game. . . . That's the back of the cottage in Church Row where the old woman lived who was so cracked about animals. She had the place full of lame dogs and mangy cats, and birds in cages. The children used to catch sparrows and sell them to her for sixpence; and she was always safe to buy anything queer, like a newt or a hedgehog. She must have had money from somewhere to feed them all. She used to nurse the creatures up and say she'd let them go when they were well again; but she always got too fond of them and kept them as pets. The smell of the place was awful. And the birds used to get out of the cages, and the cats used to eat them. I remember her complaining about that to me once, as if it had been a great surprise. I don't believe she ever let anyone but me inside the house, and I only got in because I once gave her a red squirrel that some boys had caught in a trap. They were carrying it round the town in a sack, trying to sell it for a shilling, and it had lost half its tail. She kept it for a fortnight. It used to bite her whenever she went near it; and she said it used to stand on the windowsill and look out, and stamp with its hind feet like a rabbit whenever it saw the birds hopping about in the garden outside. It was frightfully wild, and the cats were terrified of it. It spent most of its time up at the top of her curtains, and in the end it got away. She went all round the town crying, and giving the school-children pennies to look for it. She said they could tell it by the short tail. Some of them did trace it into one of the Castle Mound elm trees. It stopped there all afternoon, but in the night it escaped into the woods and never was seen again. I don't believe she ever thought it would be happy without her. . . . Poor old thing, she hadn't a friend in the world, and no one knew she was ill. Sometimes she didn't go out in the winter for days together. The people in the next cottage never thought of anything being wrong till a week after she was dead. A nasty business. . . . The birds in the cages had all starved, I remember, and the cats had been at one or two of them. I really believe the other people in Church Row were frightened of her and thought there had been something uncanny about her. Anyhow, they wouldn't look after the dogs, and I had to have all but the one I took destroyed. The cats were all right, of course; they'd gone off into the attics of these old cottages after the mice and rats; and I dare say some of their descendants are alive to this day. There wasn't a bit of food in the house; but that handkerchief full of jewellery under her pillow was worth nearly eight hundred pounds. I never found anyone to claim it. She must have been absolutely off her head. . . . And there was that extraordinary old parson and his wife who lived in Barbican Cottage. She had her half of the house and he had his; and they didn't speak for ten years. They each had their own money and bought their own food and went out at their own times; and they used to knock on the wall in between when one left, so that the other should stay in and look after the house. He told me that after she died. I don't know when or why they'd arranged their way of living; it all seemed perfectly inexplicable. He wouldn't go near her when she was dying, and I'm bound to say she never asked for him; and when I told him she was dead he only said, 'That's a blessing. I never liked the woman.' And he sold the cottage and left the place, and I never heard a word more about him. *He* ought to have been in an asylum if ever anyone should. . . . And if you come to queer

people, there was Amelia Barry. I've always been
perfectly sure she poisoned her mother. She wasn't
mad, though; she was as sane as I am. She must have
given the old woman an overdose of the sleeping
mixture and finished her off. I wasn't in the least surprised that she couldn't produce the bottle when
I asked for it. Said she'd had an accident pouring out
the dose and smashed it. Sort of thing an inexperi-
enced criminal would pitch upon. I didn't tell her
that I didn't believe her. What would have been the
use? The old woman was dying of heart disease, any-
way, and she'd been spoiling Amelia's life for years.
The girl had persuaded herself that she was never
going to get away, and she was wild for love of that
scapegrace fellow who took her off to India afterward. She daren't let him go without her. She didn't
trust him out of her sight, and she was quite right
there. He turned out a pretty bad bargain in the
end. But he did marry her, and I suppose that was
what she did it for. And he never would have married
her if the old mother hadn't died just then and left
Amelia all the money. I know quite well how many
doses there were in that bottle. Thompson had only
sent it in the day before; I found the entry in his
poison book. Quite enough to do the job: don't tell
me it all went down the sink! But I didn't care

whether old Mrs. Barry died then or six months later. She was no good to anyone; and Amelia had her reasons for wanting a husband. I let it go at 'cardiac failure.' So it was, in a way: so's any other kind of death." And he thought with grim amusement, "There were two people who ought to have been in the dock over that business, myself and Amelia," as he stopped to see whether there was anything new in old Archibald's antique-shop window.

There was nothing in particular; Archibald must have been slack lately about attending sales. His wife had always been the brains of the business, and since her death he had moved away from the house behind the shop, gone to live in one of the new red-brick villas on Camp Hill, and lost much of his interest in his stock. He had done well in his time out of the Americans who came to stay at the Jolly Highwayman, the motorists who lunched in the town on their way to the West country, and the anglers who came to fish the Dodder; but now the shop was little more than a hobby. He still enjoyed a good piece of silver or glass as much as anyone, but he had no longer any objection to putting a fake or two in his window for people who knew no better, and he had ceased to supervise the statements of a young salesman whom he had installed. There

was the usual mixed collection in the window to-day;
and Doctor Serocold, who had an eye for such things,
sniffed mildly at the juxtaposition of a row of blue
Czecho-Slovakian wineglasses, miscalled Bristol, half
a chipped and cracked Rockingham tea set, a shelf
of modern brass door knockers and toasting forks,
one or two frayed pieces of Victorian beadwork, a
stitched Waterford decanter with honeycomb cutting,
and a really beautiful Irish silver soup ladle with
feather-edge chasing, on which he had long set his
heart. He would have gone in to ask Archibald
whether its price had come down to his limit yet;
but there was no sign of the old man, and the young
assistant, whom the doctor much disliked for his
impertinence, was poking about with a customer
among the tallboys, chests of drawers, and china cup-
boards with which the back of the shop was encumbered. So he turned away and went round to the
south side of the church.

The door of the Galilee porch was open, and there
was a bicycle leaning up against one of the pillars with
a basket full of chrysanthemums strapped on to the
handlebars. He deduced that Miss Archibald must
be decorating the altar. The bicycle was being
watched by her Airedale, a great fighter and prize
winner, who sniffed at Doctor Serocold, pricked his

ears, raised his head condescendingly to a flattering hand. "I'll just go in and ask her when she wants me to arrange my next course of home nursing lectures for the girl guides," decided the doctor; and he stepped over the unprotesting dog and entered the church.

Miss Archibald was in the vestry, making herself disagreeable to Simmons, the verger, a doddering old man who pottered about the church on week days, attaching himself to casual visitors. She was making him carry away dead flowers, empty cans, and mop up spilt water from the flagstones with great reluctance, while she stood at the vestry table, with a row of surplices behind her, polishing a dirty altar vase with a determination that brought two spots of red colour into her sallow cheeks. She was a tall, thin young woman in her late thirties, with a hawk nose and very straight black hair and a skin so tanned by her outdoor life that she made Doctor Serocold think of a North American Indian. She had a way of carrying her head very high and snapping out at people in her deep boyish voice that made her rather unpopular. She never wasted any time in consideration; she was polite enough, but she always knew exactly what she wanted to say and said it immediately. She told the doctor in half a dozen sentences what he wanted to know, finishing off her brass vase meanwhile with a last vigorous rub, and then started to clip the stems of the chrysanthemums, which Simmons had fetched for her, as if she disliked them individually. She said, dismissing the lectures as settled, "Did you ever see such idiotic vases? Hopelessly top-heavy and so narrow in the neck that you can't get the stems in, and no room for the water. They always have them in churches." And she rammed in half a dozen mop-headed flowers and scowled at the result.

"I wish the vicar would get someone else to do his beastly flowers," she said, dissatisfied. "People are always offering to take it on, but after a week or two they get sick of it and he has to fall back on me, and I can't make them look decent. I'm no hand at artistic arrangements. The only thing I'm any good for is to keep the vases clean. Just look at the state old Simmons and Mrs. MacReady have let them get into."

She set her teeth and began on the second, while the doctor looked at her and reflected: "The war was the happiest time of her life, I suppose, in spite of everything. Old Archibald did the wrong thing for her, sending her to that smart school and letting her learn to use her mind. When she came back here

she'd got a taste for something better than the sons
and daughters of all the other shopkeepers in the
place; or anyhow, for something different. She was
a bit too good for them and not good enough for the
people in the big houses. Things might have been
a bit easier if it had all happened after the war. But
in those days there wasn't anybody for her. She just
hung about, wasting her time. It wasn't till the war
came along that she got her chance. She was marvellous then. I shall never forget how she used to run
the quartermaster's stores over at Carfax, when it
was a Red Cross hospital. Of course, she ought to
have been the commandant, instead of that obstinate
old fool, Lady Catterick; but you couldn't keep the
woman out when she'd lent the place. Still, the whole
thing would have gone to pieces without Ellen Archibald. Wonder if she ever thinks about it all now."

She certainly did not look as if she had an idea
beyond the splashed vestry table, the heap of wet
stalks, and the tin of brass polish. She had always
had that faculty of living in the moment; it was the
secret of her power that she concentrated on the
matter in hand. She was very busy nowadays, what
with her Guides, and the district nurse, and the
Care Committee of the Cottage Hospital, and all her
other activities: sometimes the doctor thought that

she could not bear to keep still. She had her golf and her dog for odd times, and he used to see her playing vigorous tennis in the summer evenings on the courts of the new club in the grammar school grounds, which the townspeople had made for themselves to rival the old county club down by the Dodder. She had dropped dancing, though; he had heard her say as much when old Lady Catterick had suggested, in her patronizing, offensive way, that Miss Archibald had not taken any tickets yet for the hospital dance. "My dancing days are over," she had flared out in the middle of the committee meeting. "I don't care for all these modern steps."

He thought, "I don't believe a word of that. A pity if she believes it herself. After all, she's only thirty-six." He could do the calculation with accuracy since he had introduced her to the world. He watched her ram her flowers into the second vase, and thought, "She should be able to enjoy herself at a dance all right; but I suppose the trouble is that there's no one of her generation left to dance with. Now I come to think of it, she's just the wrong age. The young men she should have danced with and flirted with and married all those years ago are dead and buried, and she's in the same boat with twenty or thirty other young women that I meet about the town, who've got to fill up their lives with anything but their own affairs. She ought to have been married fourteen or fifteen years by this time, and be stout and solid and satisfied, and have two or three children at the school-and-governess stage, and a husband beginning to put on weight and make money, and one of those gimcrack little red-and-white houses out on the edge of the golf course with a garage and a rockery, and a wireless aerial on the roof."

Suddenly it occurred to him to wonder whether she ever thought about Jimmy Canfield nowadays.

He hoped, for her own sake, that she had forgotten him; but he was not so sure. For one thing, there was the War Memorial, with the rust running down from the point of the sword in the winter rains and making a stain on the pillar of the cross that was like old blood. The position that had been chosen for it, just at the top of Beastmarket Hill, made it certain that everyone in the town must pass it two or three times a day; and he did not believe that Ellen was the kind to notice it any the less, however often she passed it. Besides, Jimmy Canfield had been the town V.C. There were very few public occasions still on which somebody did not bring his name into a speech, let alone the things that were always said on Armistice Day. Doctor Serocold remembered the service last year, the foggy morning, the crowd in Beastmarket Hill, the new poppy wreaths on the steps of the cross, and that old rogue Collins, in his mayor's robes, coughing over the list, with Jimmy's name in it, and the name of his own elder son. Ellen Archibald had been there with a detachment of her Guides; Doctor Serocold remembered perfectly her face under her ugly, looped, blue felt hat; the chin strap had made it look as impassive as if she had been a soldier on guard, but perhaps there had been something else to wipe all the expression out of it. She had stood there like stone while the out-of-tune bugles struggled with the "Last Post," and he had wondered then, as he did now, whether she was thinking of Jimmy Canfield. And then the aëroplane had come over, and her face had changed, and he had been certain of it.

He thought, "If I remember him, how much more must she!" For Jimmy had been a gay, amusing creature, the son of the local auctioneer, and just starting to wake up his father's drowsy old business at the corner of Market Street, with its dusty estate maps, flyblown bills advertising sales, and hinged counter where the farmers propped their elbows on market days. Doctor Serocold recollected him as a smart, good-looking, intelligent young man, with a taste for slightly over-dressing himself and tremendously keen on the mild subscription dances of those days in the chilly, dusty, drab-coloured assembly rooms, with their plaster columns and cornices, laurel wreaths, and chipped classical medallions, on the first floor of the White Horse Hotel. "Ellen used to dance all right that summer before the war," recollected Doctor Serocold. "I remember some of the old ladies gossiping about the number of dances these two young people gave each other. In those days more than three or four were something to gossip about." But after that the world had come to an end and Jimmy had disappeared from the town, to reappear for a brief space in one of those early Air Force tunics that lapped across to the left shoulder, and a forage cap very much to one side on his curly fair hair. If he did go up to Carfax Hospital once or twice to see the quartermaster in her office and drive her back in his side car after her day's work was over, no one had appeared to notice it except Doctor Serocold. People were busy with their own affairs, and if Jimmy had ever asked her to marry him she had not done it. Very soon he had gone off to France, and that had been the end of the story, except for something black that dropped like a stone out of a burning, twisting aëroplane as it fluttered down the sky some six months later.

"I remember going into her office next day," mused Doctor Serocold, "to ask her about an order for blankets, and find out whether she'd heard the news. She had, but I didn't see at first what it meant to her. She kept perfectly quiet; her face didn't even twitch when we were talking about it. She didn't give herself away. I'd been there half an hour, and I was just going when she stopped me and said, 'What can I take to make me sleep to-night?' She said it so coolly that I was taken in for a minute, and started telling her that a little bromide would do the trick if she'd been overworking. Then I saw the look in her eyes, and didn't go on. And she said, in the same queer voice, without any expression in it, 'I can't stand another night like last night over again. I saw him all the time . . . falling and burning.' Well, I did manage to stop that for her, and she pulled round afterward. Any other woman would have gone out of her mind."

But Ellen Archibald had not gone out of her mind. She had remained perfectly sane. She had merely gone on living and doing what work she could find, and growing older; and here she was at a quarter-past ten on an October morning standing among the surplices in the vestry of Saint Luke's, with an altar

vase in each hand, very badly arranged, looking at
him as if she wondered how much more of her time
he was going to waste. He would have liked to ask
her whether she felt as much distaste for her life's
work as he did this birthday morning for his own;
but perhaps he was afraid of what her answer might
be. So he merely said, "Thank you, Miss Archibald;
that was all I wanted to know," and walked out of
the vestry, leaving her to shut the flower cupboard
and clear up the mess by herself.

PART II

I

T H E church appeared unexpectedly large, light and empty after the dark little corner behind the organ; and he walked with a firm tread across the echoing slate pavement of the choir, past the brass eagle, and down the steps at which he had been married, into the nave, with its smell of tombs and cocoanut matting. He gave his accustomed glance of pleased recognition as he went to the Norman cablework round the two little windows in the north transept to the twelve carved capitals of the nave pillars in which he believed that he could identify the signs of the Zodiac, and to his favourite painted Jacobean tomb, with the seven sons in trunk hose and seven daughters in red cloaks kneeling submissively behind their parents under an alabaster arch. He was still congratulating himself on a recent victory over the vestry meeting in the matter of a large corrugated iron stove, which used to block this tomb from view. He saw Simmons, the verger, hovering behind the worm-eaten oak screen of the Catterick family chapel, and obviously taking cover from Miss Archibald's exactions, but he did not disturb the old sinner; he had no wish to hear any premature account of the verger's bronchitis, which was just coming into season and would no doubt form a subject of conversation between them for the whole of the winter. He directed his steps toward the south porch in order to take the short cut across the graveyard to General Meredith's, and by so doing encountered Mr. Carmichael, the vicar, coming across from his own garden to take the half-past ten service, for which Simmons ought to have been ringing the bell already.

The tall, lanky, gay young man, with his cassock flapping about him, waved his hand largely and shouted from a distance: "Aren't you going to worship your patron saint?"

"Only professionally, I'm afraid," said Doctor Serocold. "I haven't time to do anything more for Saint Luke to-day."

"I don't see how you could do anything better," the young man declared; and then a shade crossed his open and ingenuous countenance and he added: "Yours is more practical worship than mine, anyhow. Sometimes I'm inclined to envy you."

"Want to see your results quicker, do you?" inquired the doctor, knitting his shaggy eyebrows.

"Perhaps that's it," admitted the young man, with a wry face for his dose.

"Oh, well, you're young," grumbled the doctor enviously. "When you get to your sixty-fifth birthday you'll have stopped expecting any results. I've been working all my life, and I don't seem to have got anywhere in particular." He stopped because he found himself saying more than he meant, out of sheer annoyance with the younger man's distressed and innocent face. "I'm all out of sorts this morning," he thought, despising himself and conscious that the sour pain was beginning to gnaw at the angle between his ribs. "That's what I get for eating my breakfast in a hurry and walking too fast afterward," he said to himself, and then, with another part of his mind, "Why am I talking to him like this . . . irritable, weak, complaining nonsense? I ought to be ashamed of myself. It's physical, really; I should be able to control it." And he said out loud, "I meant to look in on you as I went by. You've heard . . . Gaunt's dead?"

The young man's face altered in a sympathetic manner, and he said, "Yes, they told me. He was a good man, a friend to everyone in this town. I thought of him when I was reading the gospel this morning . . . *I have fought a good fight, I have finished my course.*" He had a very simple and touching manner of showing his regret; something was relaxed by his words in the contorted misery of the doctor's mind. He was able to sigh a little and reflect aloud, "It was an easy death."

"You were there, of course?"

"Yes, I was there." He locked away the passing thought, "I shall die harder, if what I think is true," and said, "Mary will be wanting to see you about his funeral."

"I'll go down directly after this service," promised the young man in his professional manner, which after all was gentle and kind. "I suppose he meant to be buried next his wife."

"No doubt," said Doctor Serocold, and remembered that he would have to be buried next his own.

The bell began to sound above their heads in a guilty and hurried manner, as if Simmons had just discovered the lateness of the hour; and the Vicar said, "I must get in. I'll see Mrs. Gaunt."

"Thanks," said the doctor, and they parted, the young man to enter the cold shadow of the building, while the doctor went on into the sun. He crossed the angle of the churchyard, taking the flagged path between the twelve apostle yew trees, which were smothered with the glittering cobwebs of a fine autumn morning. He gave a glance from half-way down the path at the long, low, red-brick vicarage, with its seven tall Queen Anne windows, the spider-web tracery of its fanlight, the twisted cables of the wistaria stems depending from its portico, its delicate, rusted, iron railings and its dark cedar tree. The vicar's two little girls were playing at circus horses on the lowest bough, dancing it up and down with a foot on the ground; they waved their hands to the doctor, who was one of their especial friends. He waved back, and reflected that the older one had got over her appendix trouble very satisfactorily. He had taken it out for her in the summer holidays, the year before, when she was nine. That big drawing room up on the first floor had made a good room for an emergency operation, when the furniture had all been carried out of it and the faded green-and-gold walls had been mopped down with carbolic, and the table pushed well up to the window to get the north light. Doctor Serocold was getting rather nervous about operating nowadays, but he was able to say to himself that he had not bungled that appendix. "Just in the nick of time," he thought to himself as he walked through the churchyard. "The thing would have perforated in another hour. I've got it in a bottle in the dispensary somewhere still, I believe, on that top shelf that Miss Ellice never tidies. Dare say I should have done better to take the child up to the Cottage Hospital, but they were set on keeping her at home; and I don't believe in all this modern fuss about boiling everything except the patient. I've more faith in carbolic than in distilled water. Antiseptics can beat doubtful asepsis any day. I've done as good work on a kitchen table in a cottage, with the help of a candle and a bottle of lysol, as any of Jevons's fancy bits of carving." For he had reached that time of life when it encouraged him to dwell on the performances of his youth, and this was one of his favourite prejudices; but he did not recognize it as such, or admit that he was behind the times.

"Mrs. Carmichael was very clever about all the arrangements," he admitted to himself. "I only had to tell her what I wanted, and she saw to it all. Nursed the child afterward herself, too, like a professional. Of course, she knew a good deal about that sort of thing; she was over in France in the war, at one of those V.A.D. hospitals outside Boulogne. Carmichael met her there when he was an army chaplain, and a very good thing for him. She makes him just the right sort of wife. They're a nice young couple. I like to think of them and their children keeping the old house warm and chasing the ghosts away . . . for everyone but me."

For he had known the vicarage very well himself once upon a time. There were not many people left in the town now who did more than remember Canon Smollett, the last vicar, the archæologist who spent his time poking about for Roman remains on the hills and affixing unfounded legends to the fragments of mediæval architecture built into the houses. But there must be a certain number still who could tell you that before Canon Smollett there had been an even more remote and nebulous Canon Freer, whose daughter Catherine had married Luke Serocold when he was a young assistant, and had died the next year when her baby was born. That July day was forty years ago, more or less, and Doctor Serocold could not honestly swear that he ever looked attentively nowadays at the dim yellow photograph of the girl with the fringe and the knot of heavy hair which the sun had almost obliterated at its post above his bed. The furniture had been changed twice in the vicarage since she lived there, and there was little left in the old house to remind him of her. He could go up and down the polished oak staircase

and in and out of the tall panelled rooms, on professional or parochial business, without any sense of
the past; he could not pretend that he often recalled
the days when he did his courting there, a tongue-
tied, young fellow, straight from hospital and knowing as little about women as he did about his work.
He could even walk in the blowsy, tangled garden,
where he had seen her most often, without discovering
any vision among the roses and currant bushes of
that slender, forgotten figure with her muslin flounces
all bunched up together in one hand, and her small
head drooping sideways on her long, tired neck.
The wraith had lingered in those neglected walks for
years after it had faded from the rooms in the High
Street where they had spent their short married life;
but it had vanished for him at last. Now there was
nothing left of her except the meaningless inscription which he knew by heart and read again this
morning with a sense of chill. "Catherine, only
daughter of the Reverend Canon Freer, Vicar of this
parish, and beloved wife of Luke Serocold, M.D.
Born May 17, 1865. Died July 22, 1887. The grass
withereth, the flower fadeth . . ." but he had not let
them finish the text. His child had never breathed;
it had neither name nor mention. Staring at the letters and noticing subconsciously the litter of yellow

leaves from the propped branches of the mulberry tree overhead that had collected in the grass, Catherine Serocold's husband thought, "I must get that cleared away, I suppose. Simmons is lazy. . . . I wonder if I should have made her happy. We had so little time together, and now I can't remember anything except that she was lovely and young, and afraid of everyone but me. She had that very light-brown hair, almost golden, and her mouth was always a little open, as if she wanted to speak to you but was too shy to begin."

He remembered that short upper lip of hers, quite suddenly, as if he had kissed it the night before; he had not thought of it for years. She had had a way of shutting her eyes when he kissed her; perhaps she had been a little frightened of herself then, or even of him. "I wonder if I was kind enough," he thought, standing there in the shadow and looking at the wet cobwebs on the grass. "I must have been a rough, clumsy boy . . . a dreadful husband for her to have to manage. I didn't really know how to treat her at all, and she didn't know how to deal with me. She was terribly, pitifully young herself. I tired her out. She used to have those fits of crying that I couldn't understand. She didn't put up any fight at all when it came to the end. She just shut her eyes and let go. Gaunt couldn't do anything with her. . . . I'm glad she never knew the child was dead. It had a look of her. I remember persuading myself of that. It would have been Catherine, after her, of course, and Lucy for me—we'd planned it like that—and Luke if it had been a boy. I couldn't have stood losing a boy. . . ." So he rambled obscurely among dead feelings; he had buried her memory long ago, but to-day he was finding unexpected things in his cold and frightened mind; he went stumbling back along the pathway of his life, looking for turnings that he had missed.

"Why didn't I ever marry again?" he wondered. "There's never been anyone but Catherine in my life, but it wasn't from faithfulness: I just never found what I wanted when I wanted it, in any other woman. Mary Gaunt was only friendship and expediency, and she knew it as well as I did. Emily Unwin . . . well, her husband didn't die till after I'd got over the business. But if I'd married some woman or other I shouldn't be all by myself now. There'd be someone to take an interest in this feeling I have . . . as if everything were coming to an end. I'd have someone to talk things over with . . . to argue whether I should do this or that . . . to tell me I must take care of myself for her sake, or for the sake of the children. Women's nonsense and fussing . . . one misses it. Whatever I do now is just for myself, and not worth while."

And his unwilling eyes fixed themselves upon the space below his wife's name, where his own would some day come to be. "Barbarous nonsense . . . funerals," he said to himself. "I'd sooner be drowned." And suddenly he smiled to himself in his own grim fashion, as something turned over in his mind, and his brooding tumbled down into absurdity. "She'd have been amused," he said to himself, "at me standing here feeling sorry for myself. Meditation among the tombs."

And abruptly he recovered an odd, illogical sensation, familiar to him in past years, but long forgotten, that some influence lingered about her grave until he came to join it. He did not give to it any of her forgotten features; his austere mind had long imposed upon itself the fact of a broken coffin and a handful of decay: but these could not disturb his parallel conviction that something there was still vaguely alive. He thought of it as warm, silent, and quivering, and placed it quite clearly about three feet underground: he did not attempt to define it further, and would have said frankly, if pressed, that for all his church-going he did not believe in any

individual future. Nevertheless, as he waited under-
neath the mulberry tree, he experienced once more
that strange, almost electrical sense of contact.
For the first time it became a source of power."She
always understood," he told himself with confidence;
and turned away, feeling that the smoky flame of
his life had begun to burn a little brighter.

II

HE EMERGED from the graveyard and crossed
the cobbles of Water Lane to General Meredith's
villa, a tall, ugly, narrow building chess-boarded with
red and blue bricks, which seemed to have strayed in
among the warm, weather-tiled cottages of the alley
like an exiled fragment from a manufacturing town.
He had to wait a little on the doorstep, and through
the coloured glass panels of the door he could see
one of the General's moth-eaten tiger skins grinning
at him balefully out of its bulging eyes from the
wall inside. He smiled dryly as he recollected how
often he had seen the small boys of the alley peep-
ing through the door as he was doing, and then scar-
ing each other away with cries that the General was

coming. However, it was not the fierce old man
himself who opened the door nowadays, but his
hobbling, lop-sided, deformed batman, the only servant in the house, who sketched a timid degenera-
tion of a military salute and said, "Sorry to keep
yer, Doctor. I was upstairs, shiftin' 'im." He jerked
his head toward the ceiling and admitted, in answer
to Doctor Serocold's inquiries, that his master had
had a "fairish night." The doctor nodded, laid his
square, old-fashioned hat carefully among the pots
of aspidistras on the marble top of the hall stand,
walked past the tiger skins, and began to ascend the
stairs with the light and cautious step of his profession. The manservant preceded him, peering and
poking sideways with his head, and stretching out a
hand as he passed to straighten the dry, rustling,
twenty-foot python skin, where it hung scraping
uncannily at the wall in the draught from the open
staircase window. The General's villa was a queer,
terrifying place; its corners were hideous with furry
shapes and crowded with insecure clumps of asse-
gais, lances, and fly whisks; its walls were covered
with horns and skulls, and its tables encumbered by
glass cases of stuffed birds and plaster casts of fish.
Evans, the manservant, had long ceased his unaided
struggle against moth and dust, and the whole house

had a forlorn, sinister smell of damp and decay.

The General was confined nowadays to his bed-room, an empty, cleanly place, to which his rows of treed boots and tin uniform cases seemed to have given an air of only temporary occupation. His old brass bedstead had been pushed up against the window, so that he could look out over an angular pattern of stained and weather-tiled roofs, projecting dormers, crooked, smoking chimneys and tarred gable-ends, to the turning vane on the tower of Saint Luke's church and the suave line of the downs beyond. Here he sat all day propped up among his patched blankets, for he could no longer breathe easily lying down, and busied himself with jig-saw puzzles, spread out on a bed-table across his knees. The room looked east; and a rectangular patch of sunshine still lay upon the faded stripes of the wall paper above his Roman head, the bony structure of which had begun to show very clearly through the stretched skin. He turned this head slowly and care-fully toward Doctor Serocold, as if he were afraid to make any incautious movement, and said com-plainingly, "I can't get these horses' heads straight. I wish you'd help me."

The doctor crossed the worn strips of carpet and bare boards that smelt of soap, sat down beside the old man, and said cheerfully, "What's it all supposed to be?"

"A Roman chariot race," said the General peevishly. "But the horses look all wrong to me."

"A bit mixed," agreed the doctor. "Let's see, what about this red bit in the corner? Is that supposed to be harness?" And he possessed himself gently, almost absently, of the General's knotted hand and laid his fingers upon the stiff, tense artery between the prominent wrist bones. "Solid with chalk," he thought, as usual, and continued, "I hear you've had a pretty comfortable night."

"Much the same as I always get," replied the General grimly. "I'm too old to expect more than about six hours' sleep. Evans can't tell. He isn't awake when I want him." He scowled at the misshapen creature, who rubbed his deformed shoulder apologetically against the wall, as if he feared the doctor might believe this accusation. Doctor Serocold, however, had been long accustomed to the relation between the impoverished couple, which was one of startlingly harsh and humorous bullying on the one side, and of blind, servile, almost imbecile devotion on the other. He did not even shrug his shoulders at them nowdays; he was too old to think any human behaviour peculiar. He began to inquire meticulously about the General's failing appetite, his hours of light and intermittent sleep, his occasional attacks of fainting and giddiness, the indefinite discomfort, hardly pain as yet, about that failing heart of his, and all the little creaks and rusting that were slowing down the machinery of his body. The three men knew well enough that within a few months that machinery must come to a standstill, yet they discussed with perfect placidity the measures that could still be taken to keep it running. These were but few; Doctor Serocold came to the house more for friendship than counsel, and had long ceased to reckon his visits. He had first entered it while the General's wife was still alive and sane; but that was long ago. "More than thirty years," he reflected as he held the cold, dry wrists between his fingers, as much from affection as from desire for information, and listened to the servant's homely details. "The General can't be far off eighty nowadays; but what a handsome, gay, kindly, well-set-up fellow he was when he first came here. He'd just retired from the army, and that stout, jolly, amusing, loud-voiced wife of his was here, and the boy was at Wellington, coming to and fro for the holidays. Nothing in any of them to suggest the tragedy. Of course, he never knew there was insanity in her family when he married her," Doctor Serocold told himself, as he considered the General's diet with one part of his mind and his story with the other, in a duality which had become second nature to him. "He told me all that afterward. She had had one attack of mania after the boy was born, and they'd warned him that it was likely to come back, but he thought she'd be all right if she had no more children; and she'd stood their life in the East surprisingly well. He said she was beginning to get queer again before they left India . . . always racketing about, spending his money like water, and having those frightful rows with the servants, and working herself up into a jealous rage if ever he spoke to another woman. But I suppose he hoped she'd be better when she got back to England and settled down to a quiet life. And so she was for a time. I had no suspicions about her mind until they'd been here a year or two. It was her age, of course, brought it on again, that and the chance of Martha Purefoy being about the place."

He fetched out the old-fashioned wooden stethoscope to which he had always remained faithful, and became absorbed for a moment or two in the softly hesitating whispers of the old man's heart; but as he put the instrument back into his pocket his

thoughts returned to the gray-haired woman at the
Dial House, in the High Street, whose life had been
so bitterly mixed up with General Meredith's life;
and he said to the General, having now progressed
to the stage of providing him with his mild budget
of gossip, "I'm going on to the Dial House when
I leave you. Any message for Miss Purefoy?"

"Thank her very much for that last number of
Blackwood," said the General, with a slight flush
among his wrinkles, "very much indeed. And tell
her I'll be glad to see her any afternoon she chooses
to come up. It seems a long time since she was
here last, though it was only Tuesday. Tuesday,
was it? Or Wednesday? No, I think it was Tuesday."
And he lost himself in a confused calculation, while
the doctor said to himself, "Yes, I suppose you can
have her up here now as often as you like. There's
no one left to care what either of you do."

And he recalled the days when Mrs. Meredith,
half-crazed already, had gone round the town with
her wild stories about her elderly husband and the
tall, shy, slender, pretty, young woman who lived
with her aunt in the High Street and wrote those
queerly uninteresting historical textbooks. It was
doubtful whether anyone seriously believed the

worst of her accusations against the two poor
wretches, who had at most been discerned walking
once or twice together in the rain, lending each
other volumes of memoirs, for which they shared a
quiet taste, and occasionally discussing things together at tea parties as to which they became silent
when anyone else approached them. "But the old
women must get their heads together about something in a place like this," reflected Doctor Serocold.
"I've never been able to make up my mind that there
was anything in it. I did see them walking together
once myself, in that bluebell wood over at Holt
Abbas when I was driving up to Coldharbour in the
dog cart. They never noticed me, and they looked
—well, as if there was no one left alive in the world
except themselves, somehow. . . . But I dare say it
was all my fancy. They behaved in a perfectly ordinary way when they met in public . . . were a bit too
polite and detached, if anything. And he was an
angel to his wife . . . nobody except myself ever knew
how she treated him at home. She was all right
when there were people about, and didn't give herself away; but she was a fiend in private. I don't
know how he stood her rages and her accusations.
He didn't even tell me till later what he'd had to go

through. A pity, that; I'd have found ways to quiet
her. Sometimes he didn't dare to let himself sleep
for three or four nights and days together, for fear
she'd kill herself or him. . . . He couldn't have the
boy in the house . . . sent him off somewhere for
the holidays, I remember. And he thought she was
getting better . . . they're so cunning . . . and dropped
off to sleep one night; and she pulled down one of
his Gurkha knives from the dining-room wall and
went out into the street in her nightgown to look for
Martha. Lucky for everyone that Purvis was outside the surgery, waiting to take the mare when I
came in, and gossiping with Sergeant Ritchie and
one of the other constables. They managed to get
hold of her, and a fine time they had of it. When I
got back from that maternity case at Valley Farm
I found all three of them in the surgery, trying to tie
her up. She was a big, stout, vigorous woman at the
best of times, and in an attack of raving mania she
was about as much as they could manage. Especially
as Ritchie had nearly had his left thumb cut off getting the knife away from her. A beastly weapon,
about two feet long, with an edge on it like a razor.
I can't think why the General had ever kept it about,
but I suppose he'd forgotten it was there, he's got
such a lot of junk. I had to stitch the thumb on again

as soon as I'd given Mrs. Meredith enough hyoscine
to knock her out; and then I had to deal with the
General. He turned up looking for his wife, in a
frightful state . . . thought it was all his own fault
for not having watched her better. I remember the
three other men all mopping their foreheads in the
dispensary and whispering together while I told him
what had happened. Ritchie had turned green when
it was all over, and the others were giving him the
dispensary brandy; and Mrs. Meredith was gurgling
and snorting on my couch in the consulting room,
with their overcoats wrapped round her and her
mouth wide open and dribbling. She looked as if
she were dead drunk; I remember how her husband
could hardly look at her. We got her away to the
asylum before she came round, but of course the
story was all over the town next day; and Martha
and he were in it, up to the neck. I don't suppose
people believed half what they were saying, but it
was great fun for the town. All the old ladies apparently expected the General to run away with Martha,
and when he didn't they said he was only waiting
till his wife died to marry her. But she didn't die,
and she didn't come back to the town. She went on
living in that asylum for twenty years . . . if you
can call it living. She never recognized her husband

again. He went on living in this uncomfortable
house, and stinting himself to pay for her keep and
medical attendance, and his son's education, and
going to visit her once a quarter. A hard life. . . .
Not so bad while he had the boy; but when he grew
up and went into the Indian army, and only came
home on leave once in a blue moon, it must have
been heavy going. Still, the old man never complained. I haven't seen the Major now for five years,
not since he came back to marry Elizabeth Unwin.
She's been home on leave with the children, but
he hasn't. I suppose it's too expensive for them
all to come, or else he prefers his shooting trips to
Kashmir. He'd got very stout when I saw him last,
and I found him duller than ever. I don't know how
Elizabeth stands him. . . . And Mrs. Meredith has
died at last, but too late to do the General any good.
Here he is, just an infirm old invalid, dependent on
this man of his for everything. He only wants quiet,
and warmth, and comfort. And there's Martha living by herself down at the Dial House, wrapped
up in her dull historical textbooks. I don't suppose
they pay particularly well, but at any rate they keep
her occupied. She's never been one to make many
friends. She likes to shut herself up with her books
and doesn't care what people think of her. And the

gossip has all died down years ago. I wonder if there was really ever anything in it?"

And he remembered how he had rashly said to Miss Purefoy, a fortnight earlier, that another winter would finish the General. "She looked at me in a way that rather startled me when I said it," he reminded himself. "And a day or two later I heard she'd been round to see the old man. Apparently she's kept it up since. Well, there's no reason why she shouldn't, nowadays. Very few people will remember enough to realize that it's rather pathetic. I suppose she said to herself that she might as well do anything she could for him. She won't have the chance much longer, poor soul!"

And he thought in his own mind that he would like to know what they said to each other nowadays. There must be so much that they could look back upon together; and if they chose to speak the truth at last, there was nothing to keep them silent. "But I'm only being romantic, as usual," decided the doctor, jotting down the General's prescription (*Tinct. Strophanth. ʒii: sod. bicarb. ʒi:* and so forth) . . . he said to himself peevishly that they probably discussed the news in the papers, the changes in the weather, with their effect upon the General's health, or whatever obscure historical character Miss Purefoy was studying at the moment. "Time blots out everything," thought the doctor sourly as he took his leave, but he was not sure that he meant it, all the same.

III

EMERGING from the General's blistered, shabby door into Water Lane, Doctor Serocold crossed the head of the alley and came out on the pavement of Whitsun Street, opposite the Jolly Highwayman. The place had recently been renamed by its new landlord, a picturesque, over-dressed, efficient, rather Jewish young man, who went about in Fair Isle pull-overs and plus-fours. He had a pretty, silly, fluffy wife who wore cretonne overalls and high heels, who spent most of her time on the front steps. The older inhabitants, and Doctor Serocold among them, continued for a long time to refer to the house by its original, unromantic name of the Railway Inn; and even Canon Smollett, the late vicar, who had been responsible for the Gallows Down legend, had failed to connect any recorded highway robbery with the building in Whitsun Street. It did, however, exist nowadays for the purpose of robbing travellers;

and to that extent it justified its name and its sign-board, which represented a scarlet-coated, peri-wigged ruffian in a mask, presenting a pistol at the window of a coach. It was a collection of low, red-brick, eighteenth-century cottages, with some traces of earlier timbered work in the stables behind, which had originally formed part of another house; and it had been extremely cleverly restored by Mr. Morris and his architect. A casual observer might easily mistake it for a coaching inn. The ceilings had all been taken down, and the small number of orig-inal beams supplemented by a quantity of un-seasoned, stained modern timber; the doors had been given unwieldy wooden latches raised by bobbins on strings; the fireplaces had been cut back to the brickwork and the radiators of the central heating apparatus concealed under what looked like genuine oak chests. The original Georgian sashes had been removed from the window frames, and latticed panes had been substituted for them, so that it was impossible to read in any of the rooms without switching on the electric light; but every corner had its own standard lamp, disguised as a church candle-stick, or mounted on what seemed to be a carved bed-post. The current was provided by an engine running in the old stable, which had become a garage; and

Mr. Morris had his dining room out there, too, in
what had once been a hayloft. It had an extremely
impressive gabled roof, with huge tie-beams crossing
it, and a couple of spurious brass chandeliers, of an
ecclesiastical pattern, swinging from them. He could
serve a crowd of passing motorists there in the summer without ever letting them into the house; and
he made most of his money in this fashion, for there
was not much to see in the town, and the tourists did
not linger there for more than an hour or so. When
you had looked at the church and the castle, and
strolled up one street and down another, it was
time to be going. But Mr. Morris usually had the
house full at week-ends; though, when you had dis-
counted an occasional angler, fishing the Dodder in
hopes of hypothetical trout, and an occasional American, strayed off the track of the cathedrals, there
seemed little reason for his prosperity. He had about
a dozen chintz-frilled bedrooms to let, all full of more
or less genuine antique furniture, which he sold on
commission for a London dealer to any of his guests
who were deceived by it: his passages were full of
brass warming pans, cracked willow-pattern plates
and Toby jugs, modern samplers, grandfather clocks
without works, and faked colour prints hiding in
the darker corners. His wife kept a constantly chang-

ing series of pretty, painted little sluts for maids, who went about in coloured aprons and mobcaps, swept the dust under the mats, filled the grates with match-ends, rolls of hair, and screws of paper behind the fire screens, gossiped together on the stairs, and were not too strictly looked after to get themselves into trouble now and again with a visitor.

"The place gives me a bad taste in my mouth," said Doctor Serocold to himself in his vigorous and intolerant mind, as he walked down the street. "All very well for those fellows on the town council to talk a lot of nonsense about attracting new people and opening the place up and developing the tourist industry. It's nothing but a catchword, and they don't stop to think what they mean. All this shabby, second-rate week-ending does us no good! We were too far from London to come in for it in the old days before the war; but now that every Tom, Dick, and Harry has got something that will go on wheels, we're just the right distance for the cheap, disreputable crowd that races about the country looking for a landlord who'll swallow their false names and their bad checks. Not that Morris is fool enough for that: he looks after the money part pretty sharply, I should say; but so long as the overcharges in his bill are paid he doesn't care what goes on upstairs.

I've heard some pretty queer stories, and seen some
pretty queer things, before he gave up sending for
me and took to getting in Jevons when a doctor was
wanted. He knew I couldn't be expected to hold my
tongue twice over about any other business like that
last one. I'm certain he only got me because Jevons
was out, and he was in such a panic that he had to
have someone. He thought the girl was going to die
on his hands, and then the pub. would have been
done for. You couldn't keep a mess like that out of
the papers. He'd have had all the London reporters
down, sniffing about and getting three days' headlines
out of it to begin with; and then there'd have been
the inquest and the trial. Of course he'd have stuck
to it that he didn't guess what was up until the bell
rang. He tried to make me swallow that, but I think
I know when a man's lying, at my time of life. The
fellow had been down from London five or six times
already. I'm certain Morris and his wife both knew
what he came for. But I couldn't prove anything, and
the girl wouldn't say. Somebody had been at her and
shut her mouth. Of course, she hadn't known anything about the wife and family in London. She must
have been a bit more innocent than she looked, to
take the business as hard as she did when she found
that out. Carbolic acid's no joke. I never came

nearer to losing a case. The man must have had
the fright of his life when he saw her with the bottle.
I've often wished I hadn't let her persuade me to
hush it all up; but she was in such a state that I
didn't like to let the police in on her. I wanted her
to have a second chance. She didn't seem to have
a friend in the world, and she was only nineteen, poor
little devil! I screwed enough cash out of the fellow,
as it was, to send her to Australia when she was well
again; and I'd never have got a penny unless I'd
been able to threaten him with a scandal. He was
only too glad to pay up and let it go as an accident.
One of these mistakes between bottles that sound so
unlikely. . . . She was getting on very nicely in Mel-
bourne when I heard of her last. I suppose she'll
marry some man out there who'll never have any
notion why she left England; but, after all, that's
not my business. I expect I acted for the best; but I
sometimes wish I could have caught the Morrises out
over it all. They're a bit more careful now than they
used to be, and they don't let me inside the place.
That's Jevons's car outside the door now, at the end
of the line . . . that vulgar aluminium thing like a
Thermos flask. He says he can get sixty out of her, I
hear. I hope she spills him into a ditch one of these
days. . . . Well, if he poisons either of the Morrises

or one of their visitors, he'll be doing the best day's
work he ever did in his life."

He smiled grimly at his own ill humour, and
cocked his head unrepentantly at the rich red dra-
pery of Virginia creeper over the Highwayman's walls,
the signboard swinging on its wrought-iron standard, the waiter polishing a glass in his shirt sleeves at
the door of the bar parlour, the Italian chef in his
white cap sunning himself at the entrance to the yard,
the odd man carrying in an armful of luggage from a
waiting car, and Mrs. Morris, idle as usual, smoking
a cigarette out of the window of the lounge, and
letting her loose cretonne overall display as much of
her neck as he cared to inspect to the man sitting
on the green bench outside. This was Captain Jamieson, once a soldier, but long retired, not improbably
because of that habit which led him to spend so
much time in the bar parlour of the Jolly Highwayman. He was a fat, white, flabby, elderly man,
whose build obliged him to sit well forward, with
his knees wide apart, and a hand planted on each
to balance his distended paunch. He was sitting so
now, quivering all over with silent laughter at some
impertinence of his own, and putting his head close
to the young woman's untidy mop of curls so that
he could whisper in her ear. She shook her curls over

her face and pretended to be blushing under her rouge; then lifted her head again and made some reply which set the Captain wheezing and chuckling harder than ever. They were entirely absorbed in each other; and as Doctor Serocold walked past them on the other side of the white posts and chains with which Mr. Morris had recently enclosed part of the cobbled pavement of Whitsun Street, without being observed by either of them, he thought sardonically, "I suppose this sort of thing is good for business. Jamieson must have a pretty long bill at the Highwayman, though whether he pays it is quite another matter. Still, he must bring customers about the place, though I dare say they're all the same kind as himself . . . that scrubby little vet; and a commercial or so, and some of the young farmers, and Jevons, who doesn't keep him to any very strict routine. I told the old man he was killing himself a year ago, when he had that attack of D.T.; and he did go slow for a bit afterward; but he soon got tired of it and changed his doctor, I didn't care how many patients of that kind Jevons took away from me; I knew he'd never get anything much out of Jamieson. That woman he calls his housekeeper has had all his ready cash long ago, and what he can't touch now he's left her in his will. She goes about saying so, anyhow. A pretty determined young woman, I should think she'd taken the Captain's measure all right. Well, it doesn't look to-day as if she'd have to wait much longer for her money."

And crossing to the sunny side of the street, he thought, "Poor old fool, private means have been the ruin of him; that and the way he was brought up. He was handsome as a young man, and good at sport and so forth, well connected, supposed to be coming in for his uncle's property. . . . That was really what did for him. He never expected to have to work for his living. He just went into that cavalry regiment, and played about, and kept on the right side of the old man. It was all supposed to be temporary, and it must have been jolly enough while it lasted. The women used to make a great fuss of him. He always had a way with them; odd, he never married. He must have had a good many narrow shaves, but he didn't mean to let any of them catch him. He always kept a free foot. He was too selfish, I dare say, to bother with a wife; or else he thought he'd put it off till he came in for the estate. And the old man hung on and took a dislike to Jamieson in the end, and married his nurse and left everything to her. Jamieson tried to upset the will, but it wasn't any good. The old man had a right to do as he chose.

And by that time it was too late for Jamieson to settle to anything useful. He's just messed about ever since, and now look at him."

But he did not look back at the couple outside the window. He stepped away down the street, thinking, "After all, what else is to become of a man who's never done a decent day's work, when he gets to our time of life? I feel pretty sick of my job at times, but anyhow, it'll keep me going till I drop. I couldn't be happy out of harness. I've no fancy for sitting in the sun as he does; I'm too irritable. A matter of taste, I suppose. But I must admit that I shouldn't care to retire, for all my grumbling." And with a shrug of his heavy shoulders he turned into an alley, where the backs of the crooked houses leaned toward each other and shut out the sky. It was his quickest way to the house that he had to visit next.

I V

T H E Dial House was on the south side of the High Street, opposite the bottom of Easter Street, and diagonally across from the bow-fronted window of Thompson's shop. It was a singularly well-proportioned, classical structure of plum-coloured brick, in two stories, with applied pilasters of worn stone: the sundial from which it took its name was placed between two of the upper windows; it had the motto, "Tempus edax," and a device of an hourglass set upon a skull. The fault of the house, for the present generation, was that it fronted directly upon the street. This had been no disadvantage to its builders, in a day when the cobbles of Easter Street only echoed to the feet of passers-by, or to the hoofs of saddle horse; but nowadays there was usually a bicycle or so propped against Miss Purefoy's windows, or an artist sketching her sundial from the gutter, and the tourists who descended from the chars-à-bancs in the summer all flattened their noses immediately against her panes to see what her rooms were like. They got little to reward them, however, except a glimpse of an almost unfurnished, white-panelled hall and the shallow steps and curved banisters of the staircase that rose out of it: Miss Purefoy now lived entirely at the back. Here she had recently thrown her aunt's old dining room and drawing room together into an immense, cold, north-facing, unfeminine room, whose dim green panelling was almost hidden by interminable shelves full of books. Into this room she had gathered the best of her aunt's furniture, including much that the old lady had herself despised. Heavy mahogany was Miss Purefoy's fancy, and very little of it. The townspeople said that her room was half-empty: and it was true that she had nothing in it but a couple of Persian rugs, half a dozen ribbon-back Chippendale chairs, a very large, lattice-fronted china cupboard in three portions, which she used as a bookcase, a circular table with drawers all round it, at which she wrote and apparently took her meals, and an uncomfortable Récamier couch by the fire, on which she presumably sometimes lay down, though Doctor Serocold had never seen her do so. He thought it the most beautiful room he had ever seen, but too large and full of ghosts for a woman to live in alone. There were too many echoes from the bare, polished boards, too many scampering mice behind the panelling, too many shadows to engulf the light of her single lamp, and too many draughts to stir the curtains at night when she was sitting by herself. She had never admitted that the place made her nervous: but the doctor thought that he could tell it from the large, dark, startled pupils of her eyes, the listening quiet of her manner, and her absent, involuntary glance past your shoulder when she was talking to you. By day, however, the room was pleasant; es-

pecially in summer, when its five windows stood open
upon her green, flowerless, formal garden, which was
bounded by a fragment of the old city wall. There
was nothing growing there except a single wild-
cherry tree, which had rooted itself among the stones
of the bastion in the corner, and came out white
and golden in the spring: her daisied lawn went right
up to the wall, with its flat slabs of brown sand-
stone, its patches of round gray pebbles and flat
faces of split blue flint, its slices of Roman tiling and
its inset fragment of dog-tooth moulding, upheld
by half a twisted pillar and terminating in a weeping
angel's head. The garden got very little sun, except
at midsummer; and to-day, as he waited for its mis-
tress, Doctor Serocold looked out upon a mosaic of
fallen leaves like bronze and gold coins, which had
blown over the wall from the neighbouring gardens.
The grass was soft and wet, and had an intensely
vivid colour, as if it were nourished by something
dead. Doctor Serocold shivered a little; and said to
himself, defensively, that the old house was damp,
and that no doubt Miss Purefoy had called him in
about her rheumatism, as usual. "If I lived here,"
he told himself sourly, "I should be in bed with
lumbago in a week": for he had a tendency that way,
which arose from the many wettings he had had in

the old dog cart in his youth, when he used to drive himself about the country in all weathers.

He was walking restlessly up and down the shining floor, trying to warm himself and to fancy that the pain under his ribs was becoming a little easier, when Miss Purefoy appeared from upstairs: and said to her at once, as he took her chilly hand in his own, "Why don't you have a fire? It's the eighteenth of October. We shall be having you ill next."

"Oh! I never feel the cold," said she vaguely, peering about with her anxious, short-sighted eyes. "But I told Jane to light one for you. Hasn't it been done? We're all rather disorganized to-day, and I expect it's been forgotten." She seemed preoccupied and made no move to have the oversight remedied; and the doctor said hurriedly, "Don't you worry about me. I shan't be here very long, I dare say. You don't look as if there were very much the matter with you, I'm glad to see." He thought privately that she never seemed to change. He had been visiting her now at intervals for thirty years; and yet it would have puzzled him to recall the stages by which she had developed from the shy, slender, pretty creature that he remembered first into this gentle, fussy, learned elderly woman, with the thin, soft hair, that was neither gold nor gray, netted into a firm basketwork of plaits at the nape of her neck, with the delicate, dissatisfied face, and the faded blue eyes which always seemed to be looking at something else when she was talking to you.

"I don't believe she ever really looks straight at anyone nowadays," he thought as he held her hand. "She never seems to be listening, whatever you say to her. Some day I must try something startling and find out whether she notices it. And she's always afraid to catch your eye. Sometimes I flatter myself I've got hold of her attention for a moment; but before I can be sure of it she's gone again, and I'm left with her shadow." And he thought, more deeply, "I've always had an idea she used to be consumptive. . . . Who was it suggested that all imaginative literature was the product of a slight dose of tubercle bacilli? Something in the notion, perhaps: there are plenty of examples in favour of it. If she had the tendency, she's outgrown it long ago. But I dare say if I could dissect those lungs of hers I should find half a dozen healed, puckered scars at the apices to correspond with what she would call in her young days a feverish cold. Most of us have got something of the kind, of course; but she'd have more than her share. That's probably why she's so fanciful and vague and melancholy and has such a low vitality.

Her hands are always cold." And he released the one he held, and said, "I hope you don't need a prescription," in his gruff, professional manner.

"Oh! I'm all right," said she, without offering any explanation of her summons.

He thought, "Why can't the woman come to the point? People always think I've half the morning to spare for them"; and continued, "Hope you're not overworking," as was her habit. "What are you doing just now?"

He almost thought that he had caught her attention by that move; she brightened up for the moment and said, "I'm on to something rather interesting."

"What's that?" said he; for he was a wide and voracious reader himself and found her odd bits of historical research diverting. "You might tell me about it." And he thought, "If I let her run on for a few minutes perhaps she'll come round to whatever's the matter." He watched her cautiously for any sign of disturbance, while she began to explain, as pleased as a child when you offer to play with it. "I've found out something quite new about Bothwell . . . Mary, Queen of Scots' Bothwell. Just fancy, he had a wife all the time!"

"Yes, I know," agreed Doctor Serocold, rather

pleased with himself for recollecting so much history. "A Gordon, wasn't she? Lady Jean or Jane Gordon." He wondered how he came by this scrap of information, and whether the name had stuck in his mind because of his own Jean Gordon. "Perhaps she's a descendant," he thought; "anyhow, it must be the same clan." And he continued aloud, "They hadn't been married very long. He divorced her when he saw a chance of marrying Queen Mary."

"Oh! not *her!*" protested Miss Purefoy, quite impatient with his little bit of intelligence. "Years before that . . . a Norwegian girl he'd met in Denmark, when he was quite a young man. Anne Throndsson, her name was. I've discovered a book about it by a Danish professor called Schick. It was a perfectly legal marriage, or at least her family thought so. She went off with him to the Low Countries, and there he deserted her and she had to get back home as best she could. But when he had to escape himself, years later—after Carberry Hill, you know, when Mary was in Lochleven—he got carried to Bergen by a storm, and there he found this woman still waiting for him and calling herself by his name."

"And he'd been married to her all the time, and not to any of the others? Dear me," said Doctor Serocold, with a sober face, "it all sounds very modern, doesn't it?" And he reflected privately that he had once known of a case not at all unlike it. "Only he was a sailor and they do leave their wives all over the place," he reminded himself.

Miss Purefoy continued with innocent enthusiasm, "Yes, her relations started a lawsuit to prove the marriage, and he had to give up one of his ships to pay her off. And then the authorities got suspicious about him and shipped him off to Denmark; and he was put in prison, first in one castle and then in another. And after ten years he went out of his mind and died. I'm most interested about the whole thing. I've always wondered exactly what became of him."

She was flushed with the pleasure of discovery. Doctor Serocold looked at her candid brow and thought, "Amazing, the satisfaction she gets from ferreting these things out! I really believe they appeal to the collector's spirit in her, rather than to anything else. She isn't in the least interested in human beings, as such. If I were to tell her my modern story, which after all is very much on the same lines, she'd never listen to me. It isn't the motives or characters of the performers she cares about. You can tell that from the way she writes about them. It's the pleasure of running to earth something that other students have passed over. She hasn't any mental picture of what she's describing. I wonder what her idea of Bothwell's death would be like." He had a momentary vision himself of a wild animal biting its chains in an empty cell, or a paralyzed, imbecile creature rotting into extinction: he had seen both in his time, but he did not suppose that Miss Purefoy's mild imagination included either, nor did he wish that they should. And aloud he remarked gravely, "Well, one of the man's wives was a queen."

"A very interesting character," declared Miss Purefoy primly. "I think I should enjoy writing his life."

"I can't imagine anyone with fewer qualifications for doing it," reflected Doctor Serocold; and being by this time in despair, he asked her directly what, after all, he could do for her in the way of his profession.

Her distressed frown returned at once, and she said, "It's my maid."

"What, the faithful Jane?" He attended her regularly for the chronic indigestion that had been produced by bad food and overwork in earlier situations, but he had not seen much of her lately. She was Miss Purefoy's tyrant and shadow and bullied her like a mother.

However, it was not Jane with a sick headache this time. "No—Gladys," Miss Purefoy corrected him. "The girl who helps with the kitchen work and the extra cleaning."

He did not think that he had met this functionary: but then recollected a red-haired, plump, pallid young creature, occasionally seen disappearing round doors or lugging a pail of slops downstairs, when he had been in the house at unusual hours. "Didn't you send her up to the surgery once about a sore throat?" he guessed.

"Last winter," agreed Miss Purefoy. "She's the eldest of that Jones family, down by the station."

Doctor Serocold placed her then as the child of a furtive, bright-eyed, gray-bearded, inefficient little Welshman, who kept a dirty and sour-smelling milk shop in the slum behind the gas works, where the railway porters and shunters and signalmen had their slate-roofed cottages, allotments, and backyards full of washing. Jones had a slatternly wife and a crowd of snivelling children, of what Doctor Serocold classified as the "red-haired, rheumatic" type. They had all come up to him, one after another, when he was medical officer at the town schools, to have their tonsils out, or their growing-pains dosed with aspirin, or their suspicious cardiac murmurs observed.

He rather thought that Gladys must be the one who had been under treatment for Saint Vitus's dance when she was fourteen or so, and he asked, "Has that old rheumatic trouble come back again? Has she started twitching her shoulders about, or making faces, or complaining of pains in her joints?"—reflecting that if this were so the child would be better in some other situation. He knew that the walls of the unused rooms upstairs in the Dial House streamed with water all winter long. "None of those Joneses have any stamina," he remarked aloud. "I've been watching them for years. It's a bad stock."

"I think she's grown out of that," hesitated Miss Purefoy; and while he was beginning to ask, "Well, what is the matter with her, then?" suddenly he knew without being told. "So that's why she's been beating about the bush all this time," he reflected, with amused pity as he watched the unmistakable, alarmed, yet eager expression develop on the spinster's face. "Jane thinks the girl is going to have a child," Miss Purefoy said, getting it out in a rush at last.

He did not ask, "And what do you think?"—he did not suppose that she had made any observations for herself. "It's probably been going on under her nose for months," he decided; "and now she'll be

all in a flutter, wanting me to hush up the whole
business and behaving as if a child could be ignored
until it turned up in the cabbage patch." And he
inquired with caution, "Have you spoken to the
girl about it?"

"Yes, I did," admitted Miss Purefoy, looking
agitated.

"And what did she say?"

"She admitted it was true." He wondered grimly
what the scene had been like. Probably Miss Purefoy
had been the most embarrassed of the two. She was
continuing now, in a shamefaced manner, "I never
dreamt of anything of the kind. She's been with me
a year now, and she always seemed so quiet and shy.
I can't think how it happened."

"I don't suppose you can," said the doctor to himself dryly; and then thought, with repentant amusement, "But after all, there was a time, if all those
tales were true, when you could have understood it
quite easily. I suppose you've forgotten all about
that now." Even if she did go to see the old General,
he decided, it was only to talk about the weather.
And he asked aloud, "How old is the girl?"

"She isn't eighteen yet."

He thought, "Poor little wretch!"

V

MISS PUREFOY was wandering on in her absent-minded way, "I told her you would see her. She didn't want you to at first, and cried a good deal, but afterward she came round. I said that if she stayed here she must be properly looked after."

He was startled by this and said, "Is she going to stay here?" Apparently he had been mistaken about Miss Purefoy's attitude.

"Well, for a little longer, at any rate," said she, looking down and blushing unbecomingly. "Later on perhaps you could tell me of some place where I could send her, or she could stop with me, and you could look after her, if you would. Perhaps that might be best. I don't like to think of her among strangers."

Somewhat bewildered by all this, he said, "You're being very good to the girl, but don't you think it would be best for her to get away to a new place where she isn't known? People will rather point at her in a small town like this, where she's lived all her life. Though probably," he added to himself, "they'll only say that this is just what they expected."

Miss Purefoy, however, colouring and stammering a little in her eagerness, protested, "That's just it. She's lived here all her life. She can't bear the idea of going away."

"Won't her mother have her back?" inquired Doctor Serocold, who was unable to believe that Mrs. Jones would take the matter very seriously.

"Oh, she would," agreed Miss Purefoy doubtfully. "But it's such a horried little house, always so dirty and untidy, and there are all those brothers and sisters running about. I don't think Gladys would be at all comfortable there. She doesn't seem to want to go back, and when I saw Mrs. Jones yesterday she cried, and told me she wasn't strong herself and couldn't manage any extra work. She said God would reward me if I kept Gladys." A faint distaste was reflected from her tone to Doctor Serocold's mind, and he said to himself irritably, "There seems to have been a good deal of crying all round," for years of experience had not inured him to such lamentations. "Naturally that wretched little Mrs. Jones is delighted to push her good-for-nothing daughter on to poor Miss Purefoy, and persuade her that she's got a responsibility in the matter. Why can't the Joneses keep their own girl out of mischief?" And he asked, "Would the grandmother take the child later on, if the girl's coming back into service?"

Miss Purefoy looked still more doubtful and said, "I don't think Mrs. Jones is a very good person to bring up a child. None of her own seem to me to have turned out very well."

"No, they're a poor lot," agreed the doctor out of his experience of the family, and decided that Miss Purefoy was evidently going to be saddled with the whole business. He felt impatient about it all and said, "Well, let's have the girl down." He added, "I take it there's no question of the man marrying her, or you'd have spoken of it," though he felt that she was muddle-headed enough to have left out any essential point.

She told him, however, with a placidity which rather astonished him:

"Oh, it's not that sort of business at all. She won't say who he was, but she told us he'd gone to India. He was a soldier up at the camp."

The doctor gave a sort of groan of enlightenment, for this was an old story to him. He had long ago accepted it as an inevitable factor in the life of the town. He could have named a dozen other children in his practice who owed their existence to the fact that the Air Ministry had approved of the wide chalk downs beyond the Roman camp as a flying ground. Miss Purefoy summed it all up in a few vague but comprehensive sentences. "She always went bicycling up that way on Sundays. I couldn't say anything when she'd saved up her wages to buy it by instalments. I used to tell her how nice the evening services were at Saint Luke's, and let her out in time to go to them, even when Jane was having her afternoon off. But Jane says now that she always went off along the camp road. And the summer evenings are so long, now that the daylight saving bill's come in."

Doctor Serocold did not know whether to smile or sigh at this attempt to explain the matter, which seemed to him to breathe a wistful tolerance sprung from envy and from memory. He said absently, "Yes, they go farther afield nowadays. It used to be strolling down Castle Lane, carving their names on the beech trees, and sitting up in the ruins afterward; but now they can race all over the country, pillion-riding. And the camp has upset the balance thoroughly. The best thing you can say for it is that it brings new blood into the town. There used to be too much in-breeding." He pulled himself together there, realizing that he could hardly expect Miss

Purefoy to appreciate so professional an argument. Fortunately for him she did not appear to be listening; she seldom was nowadays.

She said, "Well, I hope you'll find everything going on all right," and then she said, with a foolish, touching smile, "It'll be odd, having a child in the house."

He stood opposite to her in the dim, cold, green-panelled room with its creeping flavour of decay, and was suddenly enlightened by the thought, "That's it, of course: she wants a child to fuss over . . . has done all these years. I see it now. Why didn't I guess before? It'll do her all the good in the world, be better for her than a dozen of her books." It struck him as ironical that he should be regarding all those honeysuckle evenings as Fate's attempt to provide Miss Purefoy with a new interest in life. He thought, "What a piece of luck for the little Jones slut, and what a shame that things should turn out so perfectly for her!" And then he felt ashamed of his own cynicism, and said to himself, "Well, somebody may as well get some good out the business. If the girl doesn't, Miss Purefoy will. I don't see the beauty in it because I'm getting old and snarling."

And he said to Miss Purefoy, "Let me have a look at her."

She brought the Welsh girl down to him. Her pale, plump face was blotched with crying; she looked untidy, sullen, and furtive and he had difficulty in getting her to answer his questions. Once at least he felt certain that she was lying. She did, however, seem grateful to Miss Purefoy, and anxious to stay with her, and she responded with a faint glimmer of interest to his talk about the child. He did not think that she had done, or would do, anything to prevent its survival: she seemed too stupid or too indifferent for that. He said to the two of them, "You'd better talk to Nurse Henry" (the district nurse, and a very capable, determined little person). "She'll tell you all the things to get in the way of an outfit." For it struck the practical corner of his mind that if shopping were needed, Miss Purefoy might as well have the enjoyment of it. He had observed that women like fussing over infants' clothes, and would amuse themselves by the hour with the design of a rosebud cot-ruffle, or an embroidered robe. "I suppose a needle *is* a substitute for a pipe, when it comes to nerves," he thought skeptically. "Makes 'em content to sit still." And he suggested that Miss Purefoy might teach the Welsh girl to sew. "Though it's more likely that the child can teach you," he reflected, with an eye for her inky right hand.

When the girl had dressed herself again with clumsy fingers and gone sniffling away, he said to Miss Purefoy, "There doesn't seem much wrong there. One can't get a straight answer out of a girl like that, but I should say the child will be born about the beginning of March. We shall see how she gets on. I don't want her to develop that old Saint Vitus's dance again. This sort of upset is rather likely to bring it on. However, she seems fairly stolid. I don't believe she'll work herself up about the business, especially if she feels that she's got someone like yourself to look after her. But she'll need watching." He paused, and realized with something of a shock that in all these arrangements for the future he had been assuming his own continuance in practice for at least another six months, and he amended lamely, "Of course my assistant can really do anything that's necessary."

Miss Purefoy looked startled and said, "Oh, but I shouldn't want to have anyone but you. I shouldn't feel happy."

He said, awkwardly, "A girl in that position often prefers a woman doctor. Miss Gordon is very competent."

"I'm sure she is," agreed Miss Purefoy hastily. "She looks so nice, too. But I can't help it, Doctor.

I'm very old-fashioned, I know. I don't really feel
the same confidence in a woman."

She glanced anxiously from side to side, blinking
her eyelids and biting her lips, and he thought with
fatigue, "Why don't women trust each other more?
You'd think one with her intelligence and education
would be more broad-minded. Well, I can't start
arguing that now. Time enough for a campaign
about Jean Gordon when I'm sure that she's going
to stay on here, and that I am." He knew that he
was letting an opportunity slip but he felt old and
tired after his broken night, and the chill of the un-
warmed room seemed suddenly to be eating into
his very bones. He gave up a sentence which should
have begun, "A sensible woman like you ought to
take a different line," and mumbled instead, "Well,
I'm sure everything will be all right. Is there anything more that I can do for you before I go? I'm
due at the town hall at twelve, you know."

She had begun, however, to make a defense of her
own, of which the first words had escaped him, and
when he stopped speaking he found her half-way
through a sentence which ended, "You know, none
of your old patients can bear to go to anyone but
you."

Her bright and anxious eyes seemed to reproach

him, as he said rather vexedly, "I'm getting out of date. I dare say there are plenty of people who would like a change." He told himself sulkily, even as he said it, "I'm only trying to make her contradict me . . . childish." But if he was, he succeeded, for she burst out at him with innocent distress, "How can you say so? Why, you're part of our lives!"

It fairly silenced him, and she continued, as if she were determined to shame him out of his ill temper, "Of course we couldn't do without you, Doctor Serocold. Think, you've been here as long as most of us can remember! You know everything about us. We don't have to explain our bodies or our minds to you. We don't need to tell you how old we are, or how poor, or how worried; you've heard it all years before. We just come to you whenever there's anything wrong; we know that you'll help us if you can, and that if there's no help, at any rate you'll understand. You've been through all our troubles with us. How can we feel the same about a stranger?"

He could not find any reply; he wondered if he dared force his tired mind to believe her. "Women living alone always turn romantic about the doctor or the parson," he told himself bitterly. "We're the only men they see. I'm simply letting myself be flattered." And then he thought, "But if it were true it would make up to me for some of the things I've missed. I told myself this morning that I hadn't done much with my life, but perhaps I've done more than I know."

Miss Purefoy had been overcome by her old shyness; she began to stammer that it was late and that she was wasting his time; and he absently allowed her to hurry him through her pale, empty hall, with its arched recesses and classical busts. She opened the door for him herself, and as he said goodbye to her between the wrought-iron torch extinguishers under the shell-shaped, leaded hood where the swallows nested yearly, he was moved by a remorseful impulse to say to her, "You know, I think you're being too kind to that wretched little Welsh girl."

She blushed painfully and said, "I'm just doing something to please myself. I don't feel as if my life were very useful to anyone nowadays."

It was so odd an echo of the mood which had weighed upon him all the morning that he was ashamed to pity her for it. He only shook her hand more kindly than he had done for years and said, "We all get that idea sometimes. But it doesn't do for us to add up sums before they're finished." It made her smile, which was all that it had been meant to do; but it came back to him as a piece of advice that might apply to himself sometime after he had left her. "Perhaps I'm getting my own answer wrong," he thought, as he walked along the High Street by himself, hunching his shoulders into his overcoat, and wishing that the autumn sun, for all its gold, had a little more strength in it.

PART III

I

A FEW yards along in the gutter he observed his friend, Miss Van Ness, the American artist, sketching the outside of the Dial House, and looking like a moulting parrot in the medley of bright-coloured scarves, coats, and shawls in which she always involved her chilly little person when she was painting out of doors. She sat huddled together on her camp stool, with her feet crossed under her, and her head sunk into her shoulder in a birdlike fashion; her claw-like hand darted at the canvas as she blinked her eyes against the light. She was a tiny, dainty, excitable old woman, rich, travelled, and amusing; for the last two summers she had stayed at the Jolly Highwayman because she had friends in the neighbourhood and found the country paintable; but the first breath of winter would drive her South, like the twittering swallows she resembled. Only an exceptionally warm sequence of days could be keeping her now. Doctor Serocold imagined that her trunks were all ready packed in her bedroom at the inn, and that any day he might wake up and find her flown. She waved a paint brush at him arrestingly and called out before he reached her, "Isn't this just golden? Look at the colour of that roof in the sun."

"It's what the country people round here call Saint Luke's summer," said he, looking at her picture, which was just emerging from the charcoal stage. "A bit of warmth we always get just before the winter comes."

"That sounds great, but what has he to do with it?"

"It's his day to-day. He's the patron saint of doctors. I suppose that's why I was called after him. It's my birthday, too." He thought this might amuse her, and apparently it did.

"Then this ought to be your lucky day," she suggested, cocking her head on one side like a considering bird. She was sharp enough, moreover, to catch the tremor in his face as he reflected, "Not very lucky, if I get the sort of letter I expect to-night." He answered grimly, "That remains to be seen. I don't call any day lucky till it's over."

She replied acutely. "Now don't you worry, Doctor. Whatever it is, it isn't worth it," and she grinned at him so impudently that he was obliged to laugh. "Upon my soul, I don't know that anything's worth worrying over," he agreed, and diverted her attention by asking her how much longer the town could expect to keep her.

"Not a day after the sun goes in," said she. "I'm all packed and ready—just hanging on like the last leaf. This time next month I guess I shall be in Egypt."

"You'll find the swallows and house martens there," said he absurdly. "They went last month."

"Yes," she agreed. "I saw them sitting cuddling on the telegraph wires, in their little white bibs and tuckers, talking it over. They'll be sitting in rows under the eaves of those cunning brown temples, waiting for me. And there'll be all that bright water, full of reflections, and all those red mountains, dancing in the sun, and a string of black-robed women carrying water pots down to the river, like a painted frieze." He thought, "She knows just how unsettled her descriptions make me feel. Sometimes I long to get out of all this."

"Ever been to Egypt, Doctor?" she asked him, peering up at him like a gnome, with her gray hair straggling round her clever, delicate face. It had at a distance a young girl's freshness, but when you came closer it was ravaged like an actor's face by a fine meshwork of wrinkles. Doctor Serocold thought, "I should like very much to know exactly how old she is," and replied absently, "Not Egypt. The only time I ever was out of England was a voyage I did as ship's doctor to the West Indies, just after I qualified. It must be more than forty years ago." And he sighed a little over his addition sum. "I've been here ever since," he admitted.

"All those ducky little islands," said Miss Van Ness, dreamily, infected by his look of reminiscence. "Sticking up out of that streaky, blue-and-green water, with their heads in the clouds, waving palm trees at you. How would you like to go back and see the rest of them?"

"Very much," he admitted unguardedly.

"Then why in the name of Fortune don't you?" she demanded. "There's nothing to keep you here, unless you want to stay. You've done your fair share of work, and it's time you had a little fun, before it's too late. If I were you I should up-stakes and go."

"H'm," said he, with his shaggy eyebrows bent upon her. "Something to be said for the idea. I don't know that you wouldn't be right."

"You're thinking of it," she cried triumphantly. "Oh, I understand you all right, I guess. You're just pining for an excuse to do it. I believe it's been in your mind for years."

"To go and see the world," he completed, with a strange, wandering look. "To walk out of here one fine morning and never come back! I've always thought there was something that appealed to me in the notion."

"Then why don't you go?" demanded the little woman. He opened his mouth to reply, but seemed to change his mind. "I'm past all that," he said heavily. "I'm just an old cart horse in harness, nowadays: I shall die between the shafts." And he thought, "I can't explain to her. She's got no roots." The single, detached phrase floated in his mind and seemed to explain her to him, but he had no words for the feeling that had kept him rooted in this small town throughout his working life, with but few intervals of dissatisfaction or regret. "I suppose I haven't any taste for adventure," he decided rebelliously. "I've stuck on doing the same thing year after year . . . getting always a little less enterprising and a little less keen . . . losing my ambition if ever I had any . . . just getting through my work. It must seem dull to a woman like her. But it hasn't been so damned dull as all that; I've had my compensations."

And he said good-bye to Miss Van Ness and went on toward the town hall. Walking along the east pavement of the High Street with the sun casting his shadow before him, it seemed to his sharpened perceptions that he looked at the place for the first time, appreciating as a stranger might have done the ranged formality of the brown, white, and gray houses, with their modern shop fronts over-hung by bulging Regency bow windows, supported on Ionic columns, or by projecting timbered upper stories, whose carved beams were disguised by centuries of paint. In between the shops were crowded brick cottages, with neat green doors, whose thresholds were below street level, and small latticed windows which no one yet had troubled to enlarge. Above, the receding planes of the tiled and mossy roofs, golden with lichen and tufted with house-leek cushions, accepted the October sunshine with a mild satisfaction. He thought, "It's a pleasant place to live in, after all."

It was market day, and the open space at the top of Beastmarket Hill was full of penned and bleating sheep, lounging farmers, battered Ford cars, and egg-and-butter stalls decorated by jam jars crammed with Michaelmas daisies. He made his way across the cobblestones between piles of crockery, stalls for cheap jewellery, prints, and calico, and baskets full of coloured sweets; the steps of the Butter Cross were piled up with crates of fowls. The third Saturday

in October was always the date of the festival called
Duck Fair, and the Beastmarket itself was already
filled up with the pens for sheep and cattle, the tents
and booths for the shooting galleries and side shows,
the twisted brass rods, painted woodwork, and
looking-glass panels for the swing boats and the
merry-go-round. He walked through the blowing
straw, between the groups of staring idlers, and saw
a mangy lion yawning at him out of its cage on a
wagon as it was drawn through the crowd, and he
remembered with amusement how once, returning
from a midnight case, his horse had tried to run
away from three circus elephants coming to Duck
Fair. "As big as houses they looked in the moon-
light," he said to himself. "I couldn't believe my
eyes, either."

The town hall was an unusually cheerful, solid,
and dignified little building, of rosy brick and white
stone, raised upon the arches of a covered vegetable
market. A double flight of balustraded steps approached the principal doorway, above which was a
crowned and robed statue of Queen Anne, looking
very stout, in a semi-circular niche. Doctor Serocold
had always laughed at her. On either side of her
stretched a line of tall windows, with stone sills and
pediment and projecting iron balconies; above her

was a classical cornice, and a green copper cupola upon the roof to shelter the curfew bell, which still rang a hundred strokes each night at nine o'clock. The doctor ascended the outside staircase, paused for a moment at the doorway under the carved and painted Royal arms, and glanced across the stalls and awnings to where the immense tower and spire of Saint Luke's reared itself into the October sky above the brown confusion of the roofs. The chiming children of the north transept were invisible from this point, but a second dial on the western face of the tower, sky-blue with figures of gold, pointed to twelve o'clock, and as he stood with one hand on the sun-warmed balustrade he heard the chimes beginning airily above the noises of the marketplace. The tune, as always at midday, was the "Old Hundredth."

"All . . . people-that-on-earth . . . do . . . dwell,
   Sing . . . to-the-lord-with . . . cheer . . . ful . . . voice."

He did not wait for their stammering deliberation to complete the verse. The first notes had, as if by a spell, released the children from the grammar school opposite, and all the boys came rioting out of the asphalt playground, shouting to one another that the menagerie had come. Doctor Serocold turned on his heel and entered the building.

The interior was stone-floored, cool and dim, panelled in walnut, and very spacious. He crossed a wide hall, where a disused hand fire engine, a row of painted leather buckets, a set of fetters, a man trap, a worm-eaten pillory, and a cracked church bell were grouped together for the edification of the tourist; and climbed the shallow treads of a stone staircase, whose iron railing was elaborately wrought into a pattern of tendrils and vine leaves, which quivered to his passing footsteps. At the second turn of this staircase, and at the level of a brass Jacobean chandelier, turning and twisting slightly in the draughty well, he laid his hand upon a door to his right, passed through the magistrates' court, where the empty benches smelt of disinfectant soap and furniture polish, and entered the mayor's parlour, which was used as a council chamber when only a small attendance was expected.

The little room, with its white-painted panels, its crowded maps and prints of local antiquities, its baize-covered table, ranged inkstands, and blotting paper, held five people already when he came in, about as many as he expected for anything so dull as his own interim report to the medical sub-com-

mittee. He greeted them in turn. Mrs. Matcham
came first, tall, handsome, white-haired, rather man-
nish in her clerical gray coat and skirt, and the
wide felt hat that she always pushed to the back of
her head in the heat of a discussion. A moneyed,
intelligent, autocratic widow without children, she
had always taken a great part in local affairs and was
an old ally of the doctor's. He used to smile a little
sometimes at all her activities, her magistrature, her
Poor Law guardianship, her apparently permanent
post as secretary to the local Conservative association, her perpetual hold upon the treasurership of the
Cottage Hospital: but he did not do it in public,
for after all there was no one much to take her place,
and as long as people would put up with her ways
he, for one, had no wish to see her disturbed. She
was too useful to him where she was. A serious,
simple person, of little humour and slow to accept
unfamiliar aspects of any problem, she liked human-
ity to fit into pigeonholes; and her charity was most
generous toward those types of distress to which
she was already accustomed. A certain lack of resili-
ence in her mind would always prejudice her against
the unknown. She required time to assimilate new
material; but if she was slow in coming to any
decision, she was equally obstinate in maintaining

her views, and always impatient of criticism or disagreement. When prepared in advance she was a determined, if not always a tactful, ally; the doctor did not trust her judgment too far, but he knew that he could always rely on her courage. She met him with a twinkle of her bright blue eyes and a restrained grip of her cool and powerful hand. He thought, "I can always count on her to back me up."

Her neighbour at the baize-covered table was Sir Richard Martin, the wrinkled, sun-dried, cautious, humorous little judge, retired these five years from some West African district whose name the doctor never could recollect. He was a widower with two grown-up daughters, and the owner of a charming but dilapidated Jacobean house, enclosed in a garden sombre with yews and ilex trees, and poking its gables up against the back of the town wall. He sat smiling and silent in his place, turning his injected, yellowish eyes absently from one to the other of his neighbours. Doctor Serocold used to wonder how their small intrigues affected him, after all the years that he had spent in considering matters of life and death. He was always interested, watchful, and patient; he had a considerable sense of humour, which he kept for the most part concealed. He was very much broken in health by his sojourn in the tropics, had had blackwater fever twice, suffered three or four times a year from recurrent relapses into malaria, and was obliged to pay respect to a somewhat damaged heart. He looked half the size and weight of fat Collins, occupying the mayor's seat on his other side, in front of the glass case that held the two silver Charles the Second maces, and blinking out of his little pigs' eyes at the doctor's arrival. Beyond him old Mr. Graves, the precise, fussy town clerk, pursing his compressed lips together, was fidgeting with his papers and glasses; and the quintette was completed by Jenkins the fishmonger, active, ferret-faced, and red-haired, socialistic in his views and aggressive in his manners. He was on his feet as usual, between the table and the window, comparing his watch ostentatiously with the brass face of the grandfather clock in the corner, and grudging every minute spared from business. "He's the only one to get anything done," thought the doctor; "but he rushes things and spoils them."

The little man nodded sharply to the doctor and went on muttering to the mayor that six was a quorum. The fat man puffed and wheezed, as he always did before getting out an answer, and the town clerk, who hated interference, put in peevishly, "Five

minutes' law, Mr. Jenkins, five minutes' law. . . ."
The doctor let himself heavily down into the chair
between Mrs. Matcham and Sir Richard, who smiled
affectionately and twitched his wrinkled face, as
shiny-brown as varnished wood, in a nervous way
that had come back with him from Africa. Doctor
Serocold whispered to him, "How was the Irish
salmon fishing? I haven't seen you since you got
back."

The judge murmured in reply, "Pretty well over
when we left. We crossed on Friday. Bee landed five
and I got fifteen—one of them a twenty-pounder.
Not bad for that river nowadays. It's getting spoilt.
Too much netting in the estuary."

"Too much poaching as well, I daresay," suggested Doctor Serocold, who was also a fisherman, as
he drew his papers from his pocket and spread them
on the table before him.

Sir Richard's grin twitched his lips away from his
teeth again as he admitted, "A good many of the
fish do go up by river and come down by road every
autumn. Still, things aren't as bad as they were since
the D.I. and the police sergeant took to fishing
themselves. I can't complain. It's the best cheap
public fishing I know, and nowadays I can't afford
my own."

"And I suppose you spent the whole month getting wet through, as usual," grumbled Doctor Serocold, knitting his eyebrows together. "How many days were you in bed with fever? About three in each week?" He knew Sir Richard's ways when he was out of observation.

"I was only laid up twice," protested the little man, with a sheepish twinkle. "And once was the time when I fell in off a rock and had to walk two miles home with my waders full of water. I don't need you to tell me how to look after myself."

"None of my patients do," said Doctor Serocold gruffly. "That's not what they call me in for. They all know perfectly well how to look after themselves. Trouble is, they don't do it. They please themselves first, and send for me to patch them up afterward, when the harm's done. That's how I make my money. You're no exception to the rule—never have been. Your spleen's still full of malarial parasites, in spite of all the years you've been home and all the quinine I've put into you; and whenever you get a chill they come out and make holiday in your blood. I don't know how you expect me to prevent it."

Sir Richard smiled, and said in his gentle voice, "I'm much the better for *my* holiday. Come round to-morrow to lunch, and hear all our adventures, and afterward you shall go over me and satisfy yourself that I'm none the worse. I'm afraid there won't be salmon, though; we couldn't land one our last day to bring over."

The doctor accepted this amend grimly, as the door opened upon old Archibald, pompous, spruce, self-satisfied, and mouthing apologies for his own unpunctuality. The mayor began to make those preliminary noises which served with him to indicate a coming speech, the town clerk rose to his feet, and Doctor Serocold scraped his chair up to the table, drew one of the turreted silver inkstands toward him, pulled out the quill pen with which it was ornamented, and began to indulge in his favourite vice of drawing on the blotting paper until the time should come for him to read his report. He drew a train first of all, with very satisfactory smoke eddying in coils out of the funnel of a six-coupled engine, and then he drew a salmon jumping, and then a four-windowed house, with a tree on each side of it, and then the mayor's face. This likeness, however, was not as good as he could have wished; the blots for the eyes ran and became too large, because he had had too much ink in his pen. Also he had not been able to look directly at the mayor while he was doing it, for fear of being observed.

"The man's exactly like a fat Berkshire pig," he thought, "or would be if he looked a bit less sulky and a bit more contented. Jenkins is like a fox or a ferret. Martin is like a dried-up horse-chestnut, or a bit of wood-carving. Mrs. Matcham is like a gray Persian cat. Archibald is like a pelican swelling itself up over a fish, and Graves is like a hen pecking and scratching about in the dust heap." The town clerk was worrying through his papers, trying to find an account for the mayor. Doctor Serocold watched him with amusement and irritation for a moment, then shifted his attention to the remarkably neat pattern of squares and triangles with which Sir Richard had unconsciously ornamented his agenda paper. On the other side Mrs. Matcham was making notes in her pocket-book; she seemed genuinely interested in the financial matter under discussion. Doctor Serocold, who was by nature idle and inaccurate over figures and indifferent to money, obliged himself to listen for a few minutes, then relapsed into consideration of the rack of chemical fire extinguishers on the wall behind the town clerk's head. The blue glass bottles had been there as long as he could remember, and it occurred to him for the first time to wonder whether there still was anything in them. He was recalled from this speculation by the sound of his own name. "And I will now call upon Doctor Serocold to give us his report."

II

H E   D I D not think it very interesting, to himself or to anyone else; but he read it slowly and carefully, giving time for serious people, like Mrs. Matcham, to take down his figures if they were so disposed, and for himself to think, between sentences. "I don't suppose any of them care particularly how many legitimate and illegitimate births there were between January and June . . . though Collins has had a bit to do with that in the past . . . or how many deaths either. Of course, February always *is* the time when the birth rate's highest. The population of this town isn't increasing very rapidly nowadays. . . . Queer, that little diphtheria epidemic in March: we've never got to the bottom of it. I thought I'd traced it to the boy who washed the milk cans at Jones's dairy, but there must have been some other source. He certainly was a carrier, but the thing went on after he was isolated. Lucky there weren't more cases; at one time I didn't like the look of it. But we only had the one death. Archibald will cut up rusty about the inoculations; he's cracked on the point. Still, he's easily settled. . . . Funny, how the type of scarlet fever has changed in my lifetime. When I began to practise the kids all died of it, or got complications, pretty nearly; but in those days we thought nothing of measles. Now they get through scarlet fever without turning a hair, the few cases I have to report, and make heavy weather over measles. Seem to get broncho-pneumonia just when they ought to be recovering. It's very difficult to get the parents to take enough precautions. . . . This tuberculosis scheme is rotten. No end of money spent, and very little to show for it. Wish it would come to an end. . . . Hope Collins is listening to the bit I've put in about that house of his we condemned. Serve him right! It wasn't fit for a pig to live in. I suppose he and Archibald will get up in a minute and start patting each other on the back about the new water supply for those houses down beyond the railway station. They were the two who stuck out against it longest, so they're sure to try and get the credit. I will say for Jenkins he took a strong line over the business. But he's a very public-

spirited fellow, if he is cantankerous. . . . Refuse—
food inspection—workshops—welfare centre—and
the schools: that's that lot and I hope they like it.
They all get in my way as much as ever they can;
but I suppose they don't mean it. It's just their way
of doing business. I've been at the game for more
than twenty years, and Gaunt was at it before me,
and I don't know that the place is much improved.
Still, if it isn't, that's my fault: I've had my chance.
And he turned over the last leaf, made two polite
remarks in his usual sardonic fashion, and sat down
with relief, thinking, "I've never been much use at
reports. Always turn them in late and grudge doing
them. I wish these people would be content with
the yearly one that goes up to the county council,
instead of making me produce an interim report as
well for this committee. I've no sooner finished one
than I have to start another. And I get sick of ex-
plaining what I've been doing. The truth is, I'm not
really any good at working with other people. I've
almost as little tact as Mary Matcham, and I'm more
cantankerous than Jenkins. I like to get through my
work in my own way and be left alone to do it. But
that's too much to hope for in this world. You must
let the non-combatants have their fun."

And he made his usual resolution to be patient

and keep his temper and explain everything that he
was asked to explain. He had made it every year
but so far he had always failed to keep it. "And I
don't get any more amiable as I get older," he said
to himself, with his sour smile for his own failings.
"Well, now for a little time-wasting."

The members of the committee each wasted a
little of it in their turn, apparently thinking that so
they justified their existence. Old Archibald began
it with his invariable speech about the improvement
of sanitary conditions in the town since he was a
boy. He liked to trot out a number of recollections of
his youth, and this time he spared the council none
of them. Doctor Serocold, absently watching three
drowsy autumn flies revolving under the ceiling,
ticked off his stories one by one: the pump in the
Beastmarket, from which the housewives of Leather
Lane used to fill their buckets; the skeleton found at
the bottom of the well in the grammar school yard
when it came to be filled in; the last burial in Saint
Luke's churchyard, and the typhoid epidemic of
1865. He had heard of them all so often that he
could foretell the exact stages by which Archibald
would work round to his annual anti-vaccination
protest. Nobody expected by this time that the old
man would either change his mind on the subject or

fail to express it. A general impatience appeared, however, when it became evident that on this occasion he was going beyond his usual time limit to argue about the prophylactic value of diphtheria anti-toxin. He was quite confused on the subject, protested against what he called the infection of healthy children, and was evidently incapable of distinguishing between precautionary measures and treatment. He went rambling on in his harsh and booming voice, working his eyebrows up and down in a way that Doctor Serocold had always found annoying. "I'm not going to explain my methods to that damned old fool," he said to himself, already forgetting his pious resolutions.

Sir Richard was murmuring soothingly. "I understand the practice is quite usual nowadays—mere routine. They tell me it lessens the risk of infection. I believe I am right in saying that none of the seven children you mention did develop diphtheria." Doctor Serocold caught his humorous, appealing glance, and immediately stuck his hands in his pockets, put his head back, and stared at the flies more obstinately than ever.

Little Jenkins jumped to his feet on the other side of the table and rapped out, "Why only seven, then? Why not the whole lot, I should like to know?"

His red moustache bristled with excitement. "Why didn't all the kids have the proper thing done . . . if it is the proper thing nowadays to go sticking germs into them, which, mind you, I don't say I approve of?" He dropped down again with the satisfied air of one who has made a good point.

Doctor Serocold thought, "Oh, Lord! Have I got to go into all that, at this time of day?" He had, however, more respect for little Jenkins than he had for Archibald; and he did unbend so far as to explain, grumpily, still staring at the ceiling, "Only do the susceptible cases. Schick's test is the dodge—picks out the dangerous ones. Take too long to explain it."

Jenkins squinted at him sideways, only half-satisfied, and resenting the doctor's native and ungracious impatience of lay opinion. Archibald grumbled under his breath, "I don't follow all that. I only know there was a lot of arm-scratching going on, and I want to understand why."

The doctor turned right round on him in a childish rage. "Do you think I've nothing else to do but sit here all day long telling you about my professional methods? As long as I'm medical officer of those schools I'm going to do what I think proper to keep down infection. I'm not going to have the whole town involved in an epidemic because people like you want to interfere in what isn't your——" He stopped himself, with an enormous effort, almost at the same moment that Sir Richard and Mrs. Matcham chimed in together with vaguely soothing interruptions—and a good half-minute before the town clerk disentangled himself from his papers to protest against the four of them. "There I go, losing my temper as usual," reflected the doctor gloomily. "I'd only got to spend two or three minutes smoothing the old fool down, and we should have been finished with him for another six months. Now I suppose I've hung up the whole business, and serve me right! One of these days I shall be asked to resign, because somebody thinks I'm past my work: and that insinuating young rascal, Jevons, will step into my shoes. Well, I shall only have myself to blame."

His outburst, however, seemed to have cleared the air a little. True, the mayor was blinking and swallowing over a protest which he had but vaguely understood, and Jenkins was still simmering with temper, but old Archibald had already begun to hedge, muttering apologetically that he had not intended any criticism . . . had merely asked for information . . . was glad to hear that the epidemic had passed over so rapidly. "In my young days I remember there was a great deal more of this sort of sickness than there is now. I think we may all congratulate ourselves on the improvement in the health of the town." He seemed to have gone round the circle to his starting point and, becoming aware of this, he let himself down again into his chair and puffed himself into silence, while the doctor tapped on the table with his pen and reminded himself that he had been even more foolishly irritable than usual. "If I could get a decent night's sleep to-night I believe I should be in a better temper to-morrow," he thought. "But someone's sure to call me up."

After this Mrs. Matcham, pushing her hat off her forehead, had the floor for her own two favourite topics, the schools and the nursing association. She was always inclined to assume a proprietary interest in any question affecting women or children and to resent the expression of anyone else's views on the subject; and Doctor Serocold used to feel annoyed with her when she explained to him with careful kindness how important such matters were. "After all, we did have schools, and a district nurse too, for that matter, before she came to live here," he told himself resentfully. But he listened to her financial complaints with sympathy; it was certainly not easy for the nursing association to pay its way. "I find it more and more difficult to get in my subscriptions," declared Mrs. Matcham in her loud, resentful voice, which always betrayed her astonishment at the confusion of this ill-regulated world. "People don't seem to realize the importance of the work. I feel that a town of this size ought to support two nurses at least. The maternity work alone makes that imperative. . . ." Doctor Serocold entirely agreed with her. "But you can't raise the cash," he reminded himself. "If I could have a special maternity nurse for the district, what a difference it would make! But there's no earthly chance of paying for these little luxuries."

Little Jenkins spoke in support of the idea, but without much confidence. "He knows the funds won't run to it," perceived the doctor, as the mayor came down heavily on the discussion. "And Collins is sulky about that property of his. I shall have to put off speaking to him about Meek for to-day." "Difficult enough to keep the Cottage Hospital going as it is," the big man was grumbling, heaving himself about in his chair. "There's a big debt there to be considered. All this charitable stuff costs a lot of money. What I say is, pay your way before you start going in for frills. We've had a pretty expensive year over those new water mains down beyond the railway." ("I wondered how soon he'd get round to that," thought the doctor.) "And there's been a lot of fuss about them. We shall have to go slow for a bit." He peered round the table with his sulky little eyes and caught the aggressive look of Jenkins, who burst out, "I suppose you expected the people there to go on drinking out of Roman Brook for another twelvemonth, and lapping up the Camp Hill sewage. You'd have had another epidemic if you had, and it wouldn't have been diphtheria, either."

The mayor considered him with lowered head for a moment, blew out his lips and seemed about to reopen a discussion which had been smouldering for some months through the meetings of the town council; but his unwieldy hesitation in debate gave Sir Richard time to slip in with one of his deft, insinuating little speeches about nothing in particular while moving the adoption of the report. Doctor Serocold sat back and watched him smiling patiently to himself as he talked the council round to good humour again, in a fashion of which he alone seemed to hold the secret; and wondered, not for the first time, what was going on behind that soothingly attentive expression of interest in the matter in hand.

"He can't really care a damn what goes on in this

one-horse place, after all he's done and seen," thought the doctor. "But he's very deceptive. You'd think he never had an idea beyond the town wall. What a clever fellow he is! He can turn us all round his little finger in five minutes, in any direction he likes. Look at Jenkins and Collins, grinning already. In a minute or two he'll have me purring myself. And his generosity is extraordinary. Nothing good is ever done in this place without his having a hand in it. He was at the back of the hospital, and the welfare centre, and a dozen other things I'd dreamt about for years and couldn't manage. It's not in the least what he gives, though that's astonishing when you realize how little he's got outside his pension. It's the trouble he takes that I value. Nothing's too much bother. He'll cheerfully put in half a day anytime, chasing after some fool or other . . . persuading the fellow to do his job properly, or making sure that what's been started gets finished. Look at the hours he spends keeping these people up to their work and making them think that they do it all themselves. They'd never get through it at all if it wasn't for him. Yet he just sits back and smiles when all the votes of thanks are going round, as if butter wouldn't melt in his mouth; and isn't even thought of. He's such a mild little man that none of them realize just how much of his own way he's getting. If they only knew it, he's the man who really runs this town. . . . What's that he's saying?"

For Sir Richard was finishing his little speech with a determination habitual to him when he had decided that it was time for the committee to adjourn. At these moments his voice had a finality which seemed to settle every problem and make further discussion impossible. It was a trick which Doctor Serocold had often envied him. "The business which we have just concluded," said Sir Richard, in a tone which buried it for ever, "may not have seemed very important; to some of us it may not have seemed very interesting. But that is an illusion which we all have from time to time about our daily, necessary work. I have no doubt that even Doctor Serocold has suffered from it himself. His work is often monotonous, sometimes it may be unpopular, and always it is easy to criticize; I imagine that often he must be heartily sick of it. But I hope—and I am sure you all hope—that the time has not yet come for him to threaten us with his resignation. For I am certain that the town could never have a better doctor."

He was smiling inscrutably at the doctor with his kindly, clever brown eyes. The doctor looked

back at him, stiffening his face lest any answering
smile should escape him, and thought, "Yes, damned
clever! For two pins I'd chuck the whole wearisome
business, and he knows it; and none of them would
be sorry. But he's smoothing us down in his own
cunning way, getting them all on my side before
they realize that they're dissatisfied with me, putting me back where I was for another year, in spite
of my own bad temper. He can do just what he likes
with the lot of us." But he felt a little pleased colour
warming his cheeks in spite of himself.

The committee had also been disarmed by Sir
Richard's cunning; the doctor could not help seeing
that as he glanced sheepishly from one to the other.
Mrs. Matcham looked triumphant, of course; there
was nothing in that, or in the way that old Archibald was nodding his head portentously up and
down. He always did that to show that he agreed
with the last speaker. But little Jenkins, whose
opinion was worth both of theirs together, was ap-
plauding vigorously, and the clerk's dry wrinkles
had warmed into a smile, and even fat Collins was
looking pleasant for once. Doctor Serocold found
that he could not face the lot of them. He looked down
and muttered, "Like the job," and fidgeted in his
place; and then he glanced desperately at the grand-

father clock in the corner, and burst out, "I must be at the hospital by a quarter to two. It's my operating afternoon."

Mercifully they took the hint, the report was seconded by Jenkins without comment, and the meeting broke up. Doctor Serocold found himself descending the stairs with Sir Richard, who gave him one of his malicious looks and inquired, "How did you like my bit of butter?"

"All damned nonsense," the doctor exploded ungratefully.

Sir Richard sighed and smiled and shook his head. "'It was the best butter, you know,'" he quoted, with regret.

"I didn't believe a word of it," protested the doctor. "And they didn't, and you didn't either." He was feeling grumpy.

Sir Richard took him by the arm and said, "My dear fellow, I shouldn't have said it if I hadn't meant it. Now I'm going to drive you up to the surgery in my car, if you haven't got your own. It's all on my way and I know you're late."

III

T H E midday post was in, but there was nothing for the doctor from the London specialist. He lunched sparingly and hastily off bread and cheese, a habit of his when he was pressed for time; and by half-past one had got himself into his battered old car, with the chipped paint, torn side curtains and buckled mudguards, which he would certainly have to replace by something more reliable if he intended to continue in his practice, and started for the Cottage Hospital. The road was downhill, past Doctor Gaunt's house with its drawn blinds, across the river and up Camp Hill. He had to think of his driving, for the road was already obstructed by droves of stumbling, sore-footed bullocks and frightened sheep, coughing in the dust on the way to Duck Fair. However, the doctor had time to observe Timmy Gaunt, loafing by himself in the garden and no doubt regretting the double isolation of measles and mourning; and just before the bridge corner he had to slow down to avoid his goddaughter, Margery Sinclair, who had been Margery Unwin. She was wheeling the perambulator, with her new baby inside it, up and down in the sun outside the wire cages and brown gravel of the County tennis club; and she called to him as he stopped just beyond her, "Come in after dinner to-night and play bridge?"

He said, "No, I can't. People would talk if I went out amusing myself to-night, with Gaunt just dead. Besides, I'm not in the mood." But Margery, rocking the pram and looking disappointed, begged him, "Oh, come on! It's not a party: nobody will hear about it. I've only got Mother coming."

"I'm just going up there," said the doctor, hesitating, for he was, and always had been, very fond of Margery and her mother.

Margery's brow cleared, and she said, "Oh, well then, let her persuade you. About nine."

He started the car again, without saying yes or no: but he thought it probable that Emily Unwin would persuade him. She had always been able to make him do whatever she chose. He lifted his hand for a moment from the steering wheel to signal to Margery; and then, as he changed gears to take the sharp slope up to the Dodder bridge, he thought, "It doesn't seem anything like a year and a half since she was playing in that last tournament with Bill Sinclair, and dancing all over the court in that little pink hat of hers. I wonder how she likes being

tied down to wheeling a pram up and down the
road outside instead. I expect it seems a bit hard
to settle down. However, these young people don't
do much settling nowadays. She told me she'd rather
keep a car than a nurse, and I must say she manages
that baby uncommonly well. It's one of the best
specimens for its age that I've seen about here for a
long time. I suppose it'll spend most of its days
being motored about the country in some sort of
basket, but I dare say it won't be any the worse for
that. . . . She's a good manager, too. They can't
have much to spare, with nothing to live upon except
what Sinclair makes tearing about the country, selling second-hand cars. But that bandbox full of wedding presents that they live in is always in apple-
pie order; and she hasn't even lost her looks or her
figure over the business. Most young mothers subside into a draggle-tailed, sloppy stage. But you'd
think, to look at her, that she kept three maids and
a nurse and was wheeling the baby about for fun.
She always knew how to make a good show on nothing. She learned that from her mother."

And he wondered, far more soberly, what was
really the matter with Mrs. Unwin, as he went out
by Castle Lane, where lovers used to carve their
hearts and names on the smooth stems of the beeches.

He turned down past the frothing water of the mill pool, where he was accustomed to fish for trout in the warm summer evenings, and where the lemon-coloured willows were now trailing their branches in a swollen stream, and set the car to climb the hill that used to be called Gallows Down. Mrs. Unwin had quite put her daughter out of his head before he had passed the villas at the edge of the golf course and old Archibald putting by himself on the eighteenth green in front of the clubhouse, and had taken the open chalk road that led to the camp. The town lay behind him in the golden haze of an October afternoon, with all its chimneys smoking together lazily; but as soon as he had turned the corner by the gorse cover, where the hounds always met first when the season opened, there was nothing before him but the rubbed fawn velvet slope of the parched downs, the milky hollow of a quarry, the clipped ring of thorns round the farm in the valley that was called World's End, the blue circle of the dew pond on Highover Hill, and the single dip in the majestic skyline ahead of him that had once been the ditch and wall of a Roman camp. The noise of his engine roared through the warm silence until it was answered by another roar, and over the slope of the hill came an aëroplane. It passed so low that its shadow made him blink; and he thought, "I should like to do that if I were a young man now."

The camp was half a mile farther: he saw its dreary lines of wooden huts as he went by, and recollected, with his grim look, that this was no doubt the road along which Miss Purefoy's little Welsh girl had so much enjoyed bicycling. The hospital was a mile beyond, in the dry and draughty shade of a plantation of young larches. It was a haphazard collection of wooden buildings, with wide verandas, roofs of pink imitation tiling, a great deal of barbed-wire fencing, a chicken run at the back, and a general air of having been left over, as indeed it had, from some stage of the war. It did, however, centre upon a more permanent nucleus, a gray stucco villa now converted into quarters for the nursing staff, and into an operating theatre which was passably well equipped, though not particularly up-to-date and lacking much that was desirable. Doctor Serocold had often peevishly thought, as he did now, driving in at the ill-kept gravel approach, overgrown with weeds, "This place does the town very little credit. People were keen enough at first when the thing was started: they liked the idea of putting up their own Cottage Hospital as a war memorial; and not having to be driven ten miles into the County Infirmary whenever they

wanted an X-ray or a minor operation. But they had
no idea what they were letting themselves in for.
They thought they could set the whole place up for
about half what was really wanted, and thought me
very mean for suggesting that we might use up these
huts that were already standing. And bricks and mor-
tar was all they thought about. If they'd been let
alone, they'd have stuck up a charming empty
building, without any beds or stores or instruments,
and then wondered how it was to be kept going.
They're sick of paying for the running expenses already. Something will have to be done about a subscription scheme and paying beds, or we shall go to
smash." And he parked his car behind the same offensive silver sports model belonging to his rival
Doctor Jevons, which he had already seen once that
morning outside the Jolly Highwayman Hotel. It
was occupying the very small area of shade provided
by the clump of dying laurels opposite the front
door, and Doctor Serocold was obliged to leave his
battered roadster in the sun. "Of course, the fellow
would get here on time, just because I'm a bit late
for once," he grumbled unjustly. "I had counted on
five minutes to look at my own case before we went
into the anæsthetic room. But now I suppose I

shall have to do without it." And he went into the hospital, feeling hot and out of temper.

He heard the other doctor talking to the matron in one of the airy, empty hut wards. At this healthy time of year only two of the beds in it were occupied; the rest stood neatly above their own reflections in the polished flooring, their red blankets and white sheets folded to an inch, their castors turned in, the boards on their iron footrails vacant of case sheets, their curtains blowing a little in the wind that came from the open downs. The place smelt of floor polish and faintly of drugs; its clean colours, light surfaces, and gleaming pallor made an innocent, even pleasing background for the two figures who turned toward Doctor Serocold as he entered. The matron was a tall, serious, and amiable person, but formal as her starched apron and blue uniform; she had recently replaced the very unsatisfactory person who had first undertaken the post. Doctor Serocold had not yet made much of her: he found her efficient but unsympathetic, and he did not know what she thought of him or of her employment. She seemed to have an equally polite but uninterested smile for him and for Doctor Jevons, who came forward with the loud laugh and the noisy affability which did not conceal

the wary suspicion of his bulging brown eyes. He
was a big, well-fed, muscular man in his late thirties,
coarse, hard, and cheerful: he obviously ate and
slept well, he liked the broad jokes that offended
Doctor Serocold's fastidious taste, and appeared
good-natured enough on the surface. He had glanced
at the clock, however, as the older man came in;
and after his first, suspiciously eager, denial of
Doctor Serocold's gruff, "I'm late," he tacitly under-
lined it by pulling a long face and remarking, "You
must be pretty busy to-day, with your partner
dropping off suddenly like that. Poor old chap, a
lot of people will miss him!"

It was the manner, rather than the words, which
offended Doctor Serocold unreasonably. He nodded,
and reflected, "I dare say it's all my prejudice; but
I don't believe you're as friendly as you'd like me to
think you. All very well, your talking about Gaunt
like that. You may pretend to be sorry he's dead,
but you're pleased enough to have him out of
your way. You've been going about for long enough
telling people that he] was past his work. You
think I don't know that, but there were plenty of
people ready enough to pass it on. I dare say you'll
start saying the same thing about me now, if you
haven't done it already." And he replied stiffly that

he was much obliged to Doctor Jevons for his condolences.

"Puts you in an awkward hole, with no one but that girl to help you," continued Jevons with annoying patronage. "I suppose you'll have to get someone else down. Mind you, let me know if there's anything I can do for you while you're short-handed." And he looked out of the corner of his eye to see how Doctor Serocold would take what had somehow sounded less like a friendly offer than an insult.

"See you in hell first," thought Doctor Serocold ungratefully, and replied, in a tone which he vainly tried to keep perfectly natural, "Thanks, we can manage for the present. There's not much sickness about, and Miss Gordon knows the practice by this time."

"Dare say she's quite useful," agreed Jevons carelessly. "Don't suppose you'll be keeping her long, though."

Doctor Serocold's grizzled eyebrows twitched, and he thought, "What the devil has that got to do with you? I suppose you're nosing about to find out what's going to happen to the practice." And he said dryly, "A bit early to talk about plans, isn't it? Gaunt only died this morning."

If he had hoped to repress the younger man, he

failed. Jevons merely shrugged his shoulders, unabashed, and replied deprecatingly, "My dear fellow, I only meant her looks. The pretty ones always marry young and waste their training." His smile deepened into a knowing leer, which infuriated Doctor Serocold, who glanced sideways at the matron, standing respectfully a few yards away, and remarked, "Better take a look at my case before we go into the theatre. We're behind our usual time already, and I've got to get away as quickly as I can afterward. That suit you, I hope?" He added mentally, "And I'm damned if I'll give you more than the one anæsthetic I promised you."

The matron smoothed her apron and replied, "You'll find everything quite ready, sir. I had her prepared for operation after your telephone message this morning. This is the chart."

"No improvement in spite of the fomentations?"

"No, sir."

"Mastoid, I hear," remarked Jevons, with his odd, suspicious stare.

Doctor Serocold grunted, "I think so"; and said to himself as he studied the chart, "I wish I were absolutely certain. Gaunt would have been, he was always much more confident in his diagnoses than I am. It'll be a nice thing if this turns out to be a mistake, with this chap looking on. I hope to God I'm right." And he gave the chart back with his usual grim, impassive stare, and said, "I've had her put on first, as yours is a short case. That suit you?"

"Down to the ground. It's all the same to me, as long as I'm away from here by four."

"Don't suppose we shall be as long as that," said Doctor Serocold, and thought, "I know you go about saying that I'm a slow operator; but I'm damned if I'll let that hurry me."

They found the patient in the little anæsthetic room, which had been the scullery of the hospital. She was lying on her side on the trolley, with her head done up in a turban of bandages, and her small, pinched face was stupefied with drowsy suffering. She did not unclose her eyes, though the furrow between her eyebrows seemed to deepen as Doctor Serocold stood over her. He hesitated a moment, watching her with a frown as deep as her own. He was conscious that the other two were waiting for him, but he was not conscious of any progress in his own thoughts. Only when his staring was done the other two saw him shrug his shoulders and heard him say, "Well, better get on with it." He could not have told how or why he had made up his mind that he was in the right. He shouldered his way into the theatre through the swing door, and left his colleague to begin the anæsthetic.

IV

T H E operating theatre had once been the kitchen of the villa. It was as familiar to him as his own house; he had long ceased to be annoyed by the uneven, wet slate flooring, the inadequate outfit of bottles and instruments, the old-fashioned operating table, the window facing southwest and taking the full afternoon sun, the steamy, stuffy heat which condensed upon the dripping cemented walls, and the necessity for working in a cramped space. None of these inconveniences troubled him as they did the younger man; he had submitted to them for so long that he had lost any hope of removing them; as he stood in his mackintosh apron, scrubbing and swilling himself at the awkward sink in the corner against which Doctor Jevons grumbled each time that he used it, he was merely thinking, "This place could do with another nurse. It's empty now, but we shall be pretty busy on the medical side as soon as the bad weather sets in. Last year they were run off their feet. I wonder if I could get the committee to agree to it? They haven't a penny to spare, of course; Lady Catterick doesn't do half she ought, perhaps I could get a little extra out of her this afternoon. But it's almost impossible to make people increase their subscriptions. Everyone's bored with the hospital now that the actual building's finished. I can't get voluntary workers out here, either. The young women don't care for nursing nowadays. Have to wait for another war to wake them up again." He smiled at that as he shook the water off his lean and hairy arms and turned to let the nervous, spectacled little nurse behind him dress him in his sterilized overall.

"Perhaps a couple more paying beds in that front room where the committee meets," he thought as he turned again to let her tie the strings of his mask and buckle the reflecting mirror round his head. "After all, it's a pity to waste a whole room on board meetings. We could just as well use the matron's sitting room, if we weren't so much on our dignity. It's only once a month. We must do something to raise a bit more cash. And I must speak about that new X-ray tube at the next committee meeting."

He was diverted from these mechanical speculations by a commotion outside the swing doors; they

parted and the trolley was pushed in. Doctor Serocold stood aside, smoothing his wet rubber gloves
and watching the patient being lifted on to the
table; there was little room to move, but he was
obliged to admit that Jevons managed the business
neatly. It was not more than a couple of minutes
before he had the unconscious girl lying ready, the
nurse and the stretcher out of the room again, and
the instrument table pulled up into position. Doctor
Serocold came forward.

As always, there was one vivid moment for him,
in which he was conscious, as a drowning man is
conscious, of each small detail in his field of vision
—the clipped towels round the exposed ear, above
which the hair had been shaved away, the iodine
running over the waxen skin, the glistening wet
surface of his own gloves, the anæsthetist's white
sleeve disappearing under the towel that covered
the patient's face, the corner of the instrument tray
with the lotion washing over its contents, and the
matron's long pair of forceps hovering above it, with
a scalpel for him in their jaws. Beyond this clear circle
of vision was a shadowy, murmurous background,
from which the noise of bubbling water and roaring
gas and the sharp, bemusing smell of ether challenged
but did not disturb his attention. Without turning

his head he fumbled for a square of sterilized gauze, and with it adjusted the reflecting mirror on his forehead; after he had done that his vision narrowed still further until it was concentrated entirely upon the dancing, evasive circle of golden light which the mirror projected upon the skin behind the ear. He felt the handle of the scalpel touch the fingers of his right hand, which automatically closed upon it. He stiffened his head for fear lest the circle of light should move, and with the edge of the scalpel he made the first curved incision behind the ear.

The taut skin gaped; he put in his retractor and began to clear the periosteum from the bone; when he had done this he started cautiously chipping. Each blow of the mallet and chisel raised a tiny shaving of bone; he opened a couple of honeycomb cells, clean and empty, and then he came upon a single yellow bead of pus. He stopped chiselling for a moment when he found it and glanced involuntarily up at his anæsthetist; he would have been ashamed to decide whether he felt triumph or relief. The hard, brown eyes stared back without a flicker. Doctor Serocold thought, "Yes, you had an idea I was wrong. Well, you can see for yourself now that I was right to operate. But here's where the difficult part begins."

He found his grizzled eyebrows dripping with

sweat beneath the fillet of the mirror; he could not touch them, but he hunched his shoulder for a second, and dabbed his wet forehead against his arm. The worst was still to do; he proceeded cautiously, hollowing out the decayed, spongy fragments of carious bone between the mastoid cells and the middle ear. His mind was clenched upon its elusive anatomical recollections; he felt, rather than saw, the triangular solidity of the petrous bone, with its chambers and cavities, the brain pulsating above it, the facial nerve tunnelling through it, the great vein curving behind. He had laid aside the chisel and was probing with exquisite stealth; the picture in his mind quivered with his anxiety, but it did not become blurred.

He said to himself, "As long as I can see it solid inside my own head I shall be all right, but if I get fogged for a minute I'm done. . . . Needn't bother about the facial ridge; I'm below all that. . . . Now I'm into the antrum. Better clean it out with a burr; it may be more old-fashioned than a curette, but it's more satisfactory. Precious little bone left; the pus would have been through to the dura by to-night. Talk about an eighth of an inch between here and the brain; it's less than that! I'd better rest my hand for a minute; it wouldn't do to make a slip now.

This is a job for a specialist, not a G. P. I daren't do any more; I shall have to leave it. . . . Can't get a probe through the attic; no wonder the discharge stopped. Couldn't expect fomentation to be of any use. I shall have to chip this bit away carefully till I get into the middle ear. Luckily it's all pretty rotten. I can pick it out in fragments if I'm careful. . . . That's better; now I'm in. All cheesy stuff; nothing left of the ossicles. I can get that away piecemeal. There's the old perforation in the drum, that I saw from outside when I examined her. She won't hear anything to speak of on this side of her head by the time I've finished clearing up, but that can't be helped. Easy now; the worst's over. Just a little more tidying round, and I can finish." Then and not till then, did he find that his hand had become unsteady. He was obliged to rest it again for a moment before packing the wound.

He glanced at the clock and found that he had been operating for more than three quarters of an hour. "Seems longer," thought he, feeling the sweat prick out again on his forehead and all over his body. "Thank Heaven it went all right." And he found that he was able to command his parched throat sufficiently to say in his ordinary voice, "You needn't give her any more, Jevons."

The other man craned his neck to see the result, and murmured through the gauze over his lips, "I see you do the radical operation."

Doctor Serocold replied grimly. "It may be out-of-date, but I believe in it. Iodoform gauze, Matron, please." And he said to himself with a swagger, "Well, I may be sixty-five, my boy, but I'm not quite past operating yet. You can come round and see that for yourself."

He began to pack in the greasy yellow strip of gauze with infinite delicacy; it was the only part of the operation that he had had leisure to enjoy, and he took his time over it. The young doctor was murmuring in a friendly and ingratiating fashion, "Beastly difficult op.; I hate it."

"When you've done as many as I have," retorted Doctor Serocold unfairly, "you won't mind 'em"; but then felt ashamed of himself and agreed, "One doesn't get them often enough to keep in practice."

"Seems to make very little difference to you," insinuated Jevons, with his amicable grin.

Doctor Serocold gave a snort of laughter and reflected, "You're trying to get round me, my friend. But I'm too old for those tricks. I know when my leg's being pulled." Nevertheless he was a little mollified, and said grudgingly, "Thanks for giving her the dope."

After that it was his turn to sit on the high stool and drip chloroform upon a mask—for he was old fashioned in his choice of an anæsthetic—while the other man did a neat rib resection for empyæma on a child of eleven, an unresolved case of lobar pneumonia. Then the afternoon's work was over; a slack day, compared with some. Doctor Serocold glanced at the clock and observed with satisfaction that it was only a quarter to four. "I shan't keep Emily waiting," he thought, as a young man thinks; and realized that he felt younger than usual. "It's because I'm pleased with myself for getting through that operation," he told himself; he was always sardonically amused by any evidence of his own simplicity.

"Make a lot of difference to the town, old Gaunt dying," observed Jevons, wiping his hands and shrugging himself into the coat of the double-breasted blue serge suit which Doctor Serocold considered unprofessional.

"Make a lot of difference to all of us," agreed the doctor grimly, feeling sour again, and wondering what the younger man was getting at; Jevons obviously had something on his mind, and it came

out almost immediately in a wary and defiant fashion. "Been meaning to let you know that I'm thinking of taking in a partner myself, some time soon."
He made an effort to seem careless over the announce-
ment; but Doctor Serocold saw him watching for
its effect, and stiffened himself against the shock
that it gave him. He knit his shaggy eyebrows,
thrust his hands into his pockets for fear that they
might betray him by some uncertain movement,
and grunted, "Hm . . . think you've work for two,
do you?"

He saw the young man lick a pair of lips that
seemed dry before he answered with a nervous laugh,
"I hope so, I'm sure."

"Well, the place is growing," said Doctor Serocold, relishing the stupidity of his opponent's methods. "Picked your man yet?"

"Just making inquiries," said Jevons, nervously
lighting a cigarette.

"Doesn't do to decide in a hurry," agreed Doctor
Serocold, and thought, "I don't believe a word of it.
You're just fishing about to find out what's going to
happen to me. I wouldn't take you in as my partner
for any purchase money that you could scrape together. You may be a very good surgeon, but I can't
stand the sight of you somehow, and I hate your

perpetual cigarettes. We should never get on." And
he remarked, with his mirthless chuckle, "Not
thinking of a woman, are you?"

Doctor Jevons started quite genuinely at that
and exploded, "Not much. I've got my missus to
consider. She'd never stand it."

He smirked over this, and Doctor Serocold
thought, "Sort of thing you would say! Like to
flatter yourself your wife's jealous of any woman
who speaks to you. Well, I dare say she's right.
You look like a philanderer, and some women are
fool enough for anything." And he remarked aloud,
"Then Miss Gordon will have that field to herself,
if I keep her." He waited maliciously to see if Doctor
Jevons would actually inquire in so many words
whether the Scotch girl would be staying in the town
or not; but though the young man opened his mouth
to do it, he checked himself just in time, and merely
muttered, "I hear she's clever."

"Gets through her work," said Doctor Serocold
briefly, and nodded good-bye, flattering himself that
he had come off rather the better of the two in
their intangible encounter. "Let the fellow nose
about as much as he likes," he said to himself as
the young man went out. "It won't do me any
harm, and he'll find it annoying. I'm not giving

anything away. He may take a dozen partners if he likes. I can hold my own a bit longer yet." He felt an unusual confidence in himself as he strolled back through the wards with the matron, heard her reports of the convalescent cases he had there, and turned into the office to give his final instructions. "A quarter of a grain for the operation case, at ten. She ought not to give you much trouble to-night, but you can telephone if there's anything unusual. I'll be along to-morrow morning to look at her, and we'll manage a bit of an anæsthetic when it comes to the first dressing. I've given you the prescription for that woman in B ward, and I'll see Doctor Gaunt's case again in the morning. The temperature's down now, you say? Well, that's much what he expected. Just a matter of time and rest with these rheumatic children, for fear of the heart. He always had a fancy for getting them into hospital, though; he said they couldn't be looked after properly at home."

"The mothers always let them get up too soon," said the matron, pronouncing her verdict as on a class of persons to whom advice was useless. Doctor Serocold thought rebelliously, "She's much too inclined to talk as if people couldn't be either kind or intelligent without a professional training; I hope

I don't ever do it myself. Nurses and doctors are given that way. . . . I never came across anyone quite so starched. I can't understand why the patients and their relations all think so much of her. There's no doubt about it; they never make a complaint against her. It's always, 'Matron's the one we like,' 'Matron looks after us proper.' I suppose they really enjoy being bullied, or else she's different to them. I can't get along with her . . . never could. Not my type of woman. How long's she been here, two months . . . three?" And he protested mildly, "Well, you can't expect a working woman with a large family to keep a kid in bed and wait on it hand and foot for three or four weeks after it seems perfectly well, just because the doctor's fussy about a possible cardiac complication. Hospital's the only place for these cases."

"Women who can't look after their children properly don't deserve to have them," declared the matron, interrupting him with her accustomed energy. "I've no patience with that sort of thing. There's too much of it nowadays. I was one of a family of seven; but my mother didn't complain that four boys and three girls were too many for her. Dad wasn't earning much, and it took her all her time to make ends meet; but you didn't hear her grumble that she couldn't get through her job. There was always somebody in bandages, with four boys falling out of trees and off bicycles, and breaking their bones, but she was used to that. She never made a fuss. If one of us got anything infectious, like measles or whooping cough, it was, 'All into the same room, and get it over.' We had most things sooner or later, but she pulled us through, and we grew up none the worse. We're out in the world now, all seven of us, making our way, and it's due to her. I should like to see a few more mothers like that nowadays."

"So should I," agreed Doctor Serocold, amused by her vigour, as she bustled about her ugly, over-crowded sitting room, with its cheap cretonnes, numerous photographs, and pots of growing plants. "Why are hospital nurses so keen on flowers?" he wondered, not for the first time. "They always fill up every table and shelf in the place with vases of green stuff, till you can't turn round for fear of knocking something over. I do like room to move—I suppose because I'm big and clumsy. It always makes me fidgety when I come in here. I ought not to let her irritate me, though; she's not a bad sort, and she's the right person for this job, very different from the first woman we had. We were lucky to get her; she's a bit

too good for us really. Wonder why she took it."
And, moved by some impulse of kindly curiosity,
he suddenly said, "I hope you feel you're going to
settle down here?"

He had an immediate impression of her being on
the defensive. "It's rather early to tell," she began,
rustling that starched apron of hers at him, as he
absurdly felt. "Of course, I had to sign on for a
year; and I should stay that out, whatever happened."
She glanced at him in a fashion that made him immediately say to himself, "Oh, Lord! I knew something like this would turn up to keep me. It's four
o'clock already." But he said to her, in his kindest
manner, "Is there anything you dislike about the
post?" And he sat down on her slippery chintz sofa
and tried to look as if he were comfortable there and
did not wish to hurry her. "I hope you like your
staff," he began soothingly.

"Oh, the staff are well enough," she grudgingly
admitted. "And the salary's what I agreed to come
for. But"—she paused and blinked at him, and he
thought, "I wish she'd out with it"—"the work's
not all I expected," she finished sourly.

He thought, "Hm . . . much what I was afraid
of . . ." and he said, to gain time, "You know, we've
been a little disorganized lately. Doctor Gaunt

has been ill and nothing has been quite as usual. I can't tell you exactly what will happen now, but I shall have to find someone who can take his place. I shall be looking for a man who will make more use of the surgical opportunities up here than I do."

She nodded, looking at him in her sharp way, and said, "Of course I prefer surgical work. It's what I hoped for when I came here. Doctor Jevons does do a certain amount, but except for that the beds are usually empty. It seems a pity, when you've got such a nice little hospital."

He was annoyed by her critical manner, and still more by her half-hearted politeness; he thought, "Damn the woman: she's bored to death, I suppose, by my medical cases! Still, I must soothe her down; I can't afford to lose her."

And he said, pleasantly enough, "You know, we're rather short of funds, like most small country hospitals. But I'm particularly anxious to make a success of this one. It hasn't been open very long, and I'm not very satisfied with the way it's being managed. There are several things I should like to alter. But I was congratulating myself that we had at any rate found the sort of woman we wanted for matron. I should be exceedingly disappointed if you were to leave us." And he thought, "I hope to goodness she believes me. I ought to have roped in Jevons to do this, I expect. He's got such a fascinating way with women, hasn't he?"

It appeared, however, that his own methods were not altogether unsuccessful. The woman did not absolutely unbend toward him; but she did smile, although rather sourly, and commit herself as far as saying, "I certainly haven't made up my mind to leave, sir. It's just that I don't yet feel quite settled. I dare say in time I shall come to like the place better."

He said, "I feel sure you will"; and, when he had left her, and was walking out to his old car, he thought, "After all, it's a place one can't help getting fond of. . . ."

And he drove away to Emily Unwin, with whom he had once been in love.

PART IV

I

COLDHARBOUR lay in a wide, open valley half a mile beyond the Cottage Hospital. Driving down to it, the doctor thought to himself, "The first case I ever had, when I came to this practice, was old Bob Hodges. He fell off one of his own ricks in the middle of haymaking, and broke his back, and only lived a couple of hours. And then his son Dick had the farm; and made a mess of it, and had to sell out to the Unwins and go to Canada. Ten or twelve years before the war, it must have been. Tom Unwin thought he was going to be able to keep his wife and the two little girls, out of one thing after another . . . breeding spaniels, or keeping chickens, or growing fruit . . . each time you saw him it was something new, but all he really cared about was his hunting. He was pretty shiftless; amiable and hard-working, of course, but somehow he always took hold of things by the wrong end. None of his plans ever came to anything or brought him in any money. Emily was tremendously clever, though, in spite of all her frivolous ways. She kept the whole thing together. People who saw her dashing about in those lovely clothes that she used to make for herself, playing tennis and dancing in her young days, rushing to bridge parties afterward . . . they never guessed what a lot of house-work she did behind the scenes at Coldharbour, or how she used to run the farm and the garden, and give Tom all the credit. She managed all their money affairs, too . . . speculated frightfully, but somehow managed to pull out on the right side, in spite of all the overdrafts. No one ever quite knew what the Unwins lived on, but they made an amazingly good show for the money. Tom and she always had horses of a sort to ride or sell; they kept open house and went everywhere. Tom was very popular . . . a great, stupid, handsome creature I always thought him, not good enough for her. But he was a pleasant fellow, and he could ride, and shoot, and play any game you chose to mention. Of course people were always glad to see him. They weren't quite so certain about her. She always had that bitter tongue, and there's no denying that she was a bit of a gossip, and had her eye on the main chance." He smiled his sour smile as the words passed through his mind, for he had never had any illusions about Emily Unwin.

"But then," he said to himself, repenting as always when he thought of her, "what else could she do with a spendthrift husband like that, and the two little girls to look after? Somebody had to keep an eye on the money, or there'd have been none left. Poor Emily always knew where every penny went to. The pity was, she had so few to watch! I've always believed that she was really generous; only she'd had to pinch and scrape till it became second nature. At any rate, I'm certain she was always honest."

For he had never listened to the people who suggested that Emily Unwin was not beyond enjoying a bit of sharp dealing. There were people up and down the county who declared roundly that she had cheated them from time to time over a horse, or a dog, or a bit of antique furniture, or even the addition of a bridge score; but they did not say it in the hearing of Doctor Serocold. He was known to be very fond of Mrs. Unwin; there were women who believed that for a time he had been her lover, but that he did not realize. He was all too conscious that he had never had anything from her except the bright, hard, glittering mockery with which she protected herself from everyone except her graceless husband. He had never seen Emily melting or tender; she had always laughed at Tom and himself and every other man in the crowd who ran after her. Even with her children, to whom she was devoted, she had always been brisk, dominating, quick-tempered, quick-handed, and severe in her discipline.

"She never had any money to spare for their education," recollected the doctor. "But she brought them up to keep accounts, and play games, to turn their hands to whatever was wanted about the house and the farm, and not to be afraid of animals; and she taught them to make their own clothes, and have plenty of confidence in their own appearance, and to hold their own with men. I don't believe she thought that anything else matters, for a woman; I don't know that anything else does. . . ." He had always thought that the two girls did their parents credit. They had both inherited their father's inches, his fair hair, blue eyes, and fresh colouring; Elizabeth, the elder, had been a beautiful creature, and Margery was as pretty as a primrose. Mrs. Unwin had been determined to marry them off young, before they became what she called fanciful about men, and she had succeeded in her object, in spite of the shortage of young men in the neighbourhood after the war. Elizabeth had caught the eye of the elderly Major Meredith, son of the General, when he was home on leave from India; and her mother had easily persuaded her that she would enjoy station life, which was represented to her as a succession of polo matches, dances, garden parties, shooting and fishing expeditions into the hills, and voyages home at frequent intervals. She had married the Major, who was really the kindest of men, if a trifle dull; and had departed to the reality of heat, dust, flies, fever, home-sickness, childbirth, and the difficulties and alarms inseparable from the upbringing of two small children in the tropics. "She's only been back once on leave," reflected the doctor, "and I thought her dreadfully wearied and faded by it all. But she was just as sweet-tempered as ever, and just as amusing. She made me laugh, I remember, with her absurd tales about the station ladies. She's her mother all over again. . . . So's Margery, but in a different way. Of course she grew up five years later than Elizabeth, and times had changed a bit more than even Emily realized. She disapproved of the way Margery used to race about the country without a chaperone. Odd; I'd have expected her to fall in with it quite easily. After all, she'd been pretty gay herself in her young days; she as good as told me so. But when I suggested that Margery was only following her mother's example she tore me to pieces. Said she'd always got her fun out of dodging her chaperons, and that it was much more artistic. Told me she'd always known how to keep her price up; and complained that nowadays the girls gave everything they were asked for as soon as they were asked for it. Well, she knew a trick worth ten of that." He grinned unwillingly, turning the corner by the signpost; and thought that Emily had always enjoyed shocking him, though she knew that he was not easily shocked.

"It did seem at first that Margery's methods weren't going to get her anywhere," he admitted, taking the Coldharbour lane, between its hedges of blackberries. "She was sufficiently her mother's daughter to keep a string of young men dangling after her; but they were a weedy, second-rate, effeminate lot, to my mind. None of them had the means to keep a wife, and her mother declared that they none of them wanted one. They just liked to race about the country in cars they hadn't paid for, and dance half the night, and turn up God knows when. I told Emily that I was sure Margery could look after herself, but she didn't thank me for that, either. Said she hoped she'd brought the girl up to have some sense, and what she couldn't stand was the boys all being so tame. Didn't they even want to kiss Margery, after spending half their time with her? I told her I'd seen Margery being kissed in quite an old-fashioned way the night before, sitting out in a car at one of the Highwayman dances. I didn't tell her what sort of a shock it had given me.

Somehow I hadn't thought of my goddaughter as being quite grown-up till that happened. But Emily came back at me with 'That means nothing. She does that to all of them, it's her way of saying how do you do.' I told her I thought she was a little unjust to Margery. Funny, how her sort of woman usually is, to a pretty daughter." And he remembered Emily's own face as he turned in at Coldharbour gate.

"Her daughters won't ever be as pretty as she was," he thought in his prejudiced mind. "But Margery's as drooping and graceful as a young tree, for all her athletics; a bit overgrown for her strength. How she used to tease her mother when she was lectured about not getting married, and say that she could earn three pounds a week anywhere showing off clothes. And Emily used to lose her temper and tell the child that mannequins had to hold their heads up and not slouch. That was when Margery was making such a fool of herself about that young cub of a flying officer up at the camp. She was quite off her head about him for a month or two. Emily would have whipped her for it if she could: she was furious about it. And she was quite right, as things turned out: he didn't mean any sort of business, and just disappeared to Irak without a word in the end. And

Margery fell even more deeply in love with Bill Sinclair, though how she took him into her head nobody knows. He was hard-working, and sensible, and suitable enough, except that he had very little money; but he'd never seemed interested in anything but the second-hand motor business before, and certainly not in Margery. Perhaps that was what attracted her: or perhaps our gossip was all wrong, and Margery knew better. Anyhow, she seemed to be able to do what she liked with him, and Emily was only too thankful to get her settled. And there she is in her absurd little cottage in Water Lane, with Bill and the baby, and here's my poor Emily left alone at Coldharbour."

He had just come in sight of the small, square, red-brick house in the middle of the fields, with its plain, obvious doors and windows like those in a child's drawing, and its absurd green tin porch, with the umbrella top and latticed sides, which gave a character so oddly Chinese to the front elevation. The fields were reaped and empty, the little house looked solitary and somehow forlorn; and as Doctor Serocold drove up to it he thought, "I wonder if she ever lets herself have time to be lonely. It was hard that Tom should go all through the war with his remounts, and never get a scratch, and break his neck over a fence out hunting the very winter he came back. He never lived to see his girls grown up. He'd have loved taking them about to dances, and showing them off on horseback, and teasing them about their young men, and keeping their secrets from Emily. If he had lived there'd have been trouble between him and her over the girls. He always spoiled both of them, particularly Margery. He'd certainly have taken their side in all the arguments that there'd have been about their love affairs. He had a softer heart than Emily: he'd have thought of pleasing a girl's fancy first and getting her established in life afterward. I dare say he'd have spoiled their chances, and agreed with Elizabeth when she used to turn up her nose at first over the Major's compliments, and encouraged Margery to race about all over the country with that young scoundrel whose name I've forgotten. Tom never could tell a good investment from a bad one. Emily's said that to me time and again. However, he's dead, and she's done what she chose with the girls; and I dare say it's been for their good. She always did get what she wanted, not only from me but from everyone." And he thought of a time when he would have given her more than she had chosen to take; but that was long over.

He knew the ways of Coldharbour, and he drove

round the house itself into a lost wilderness of tarred wooden barns, thatched ricks, cobbled yards between high, whitewashed walls, tumbledown sheds approached by outside staircases, and neat, new brick stables floored with dark-blue honeycomb tiles. Among these outbuildings, rather than in the cramped and crowded rooms of the farm itself, the Unwin family had always lived and moved. Doctor Serocold was as much at home there as any of them. He left the car in the stable yard, where the white cat was basking on the stones, turned his back on the kitchen door, where the scullery maid was peeling potatoes, went through the passage, where the ferrets poked out their noses at him through the bars of their stinking cage, made the circuit of the stagnant pond, where the ducks were gobbling the bright green weed that damascened the black surface under the willows, and entered the kitchen garden by the archway, wreathed in late roses, that was made of the jawbones of a whale.

Mrs. Unwin was there, between the rows of espaliered apple trees, green and purple cabbage, yellowing asparagus tops, and monstrously rosetted arms of Brussels sprouts, sniffing the smoke of a bonfire and arguing with the gardener, who stood leaning on his spade, about the division of roots in the herbaceous border. She liked to grow her flowers and vegetables mixed up together, in the old-fashioned way, between these walls of mouldering brick, though she kept a more formal flower garden under the drawing-room windows, for the purposes of tea-party conversation. She was standing now, just as Doctor Serocold had seen her ten thousand times, with her hands in the pockets of a long tweed coat, her cropped gray head bare and very upright, and her feet, in a short pair of gum boots, planted heels and toes together on the wet grass path. As he walked forward to meet her he stared hard at her to see whether he could detect any change in her small, delicate face; but, as always, it baffled him. He had never been able to find out anything about her that she did not choose to tell him.

II

WHEN she had greeted him she proposed at once that they should go into the house; and she preceded him down the path, between the tangled borders of rain-dashed, frost-blackened late chrysanthemums and Michaelmas daisies, out of the kitchen garden, and across the tennis lawn, where the lines had quite faded out, and her heels sank in the soft ground. The horse-chestnut tree, under which the tea table was always laid on summer afternoons, had turned pale gold: the sodden grass beneath it was strewn all over with flat, five-fingered, open-handed leaves and split hedgehog burrs, from which the chestnuts had fallen. The doctor could feel them under his feet as he walked obediently after Mrs. Unwin, with his eyes fixed upon the neat drakestail of silvery hair which tucked itself into the hollow between the two sinews of her neck. She had on a pair of seed-pearl earrings, shaped like wheat sheaves and creamy with age: they swung daintily from her ears as she walked along with her light step: he had seen them on her a hundred times, and always found them characteristic of her odd and unexpected elegance. He did not know where she had found them. She was always poking about in what she called "antiqueries" and picked up trifles like a magpie to adorn herself.

They entered the house, and she shrugged off her coat and kicked away her muddy boots beside the oak chest in the hall. The action transformed her into an exquisitely fragile and delicate little person, in a claret-coloured silk frock, who stepped away from him over the stone floor, picking her way fastidiously, like a cat, in her stockinged feet, which were as arched and slender as a girl's. He followed her into the drawing room and found her wriggling her toes into a pair of buckled patent-leather slippers, which had been warming themselves by the fire against her return. She had always been vain of her shoes: it had been one of her extravagances, and he had teased her about it himself in years gone by. She caught him smiling to himself at the sight of her balancing on one foot like a stork and mocked him and herself at once. "Yes, it's a new pair, Luke. I shall always go on buying them, right up to the day of my death."

"I'm delighted to hear it," responded he, and wondered whether he had fancied the slight shade that crossed her face even as she smiled over her own words. It seemed to him, in the late afternoon light of the westward-facing room, she looked paler and thinner than at their last meeting; and something that linked itself with his anxiety about his own health began to toll a chilly warning in his heart as he tried to remember who had said anything to him recently about Emily's appearance. Lady Catterick, was it, with her rude vigour, declaring at the last Cottage Hospital committee that Mrs. Unwin hadn't seemed up to much work lately? He pursued the uncertain recollection about the corridors of his mind as he began a trivial introductory conversation with Emily. "I saw Margery as I came over the bridge. She was trying to make me come in and play bridge with you there to-night."

He waited for Emily to persuade him to come, having promised the pleasure of giving in to her; but Emily disappointed him. She said, so indifferently that he was hurt by her tone, "Oh, yes, do come; I expect I shall be there." He had almost decided that he would not, when she interrupted his thoughts by asking, quite anxiously, "How did you think Margery was looking?"

"Very fit," said he, surprised. "She's got over it all remarkably well."

"I really don't think I need worry about her any longer," mused her mother.

"I'm sure you needn't," agreed Doctor Serocold, staring, and thought, "What's the matter with Emily? She never does worry, except over money, and not long over that. I've seen her go through the most frightful times without turning a hair. And Margery's business was as easy and straightforward as any mother could hope for. Something serious must be going on."

Emily repeated, in a more doubtful voice than he

had ever heard from her, "I don't think Margery
will want any more looking after now."

He said heartily, "I'm sure she won't," and found,
to his still greater perplexity, that his friend was not
listening to him. "And Elizabeth's settled down by
this time," she was assuring herself, just as if he were
not in the room. "She was very seedy after that
first boy was born, and seemed to turn against Gilbert
and the whole of her life out there. I was anxious
about her for a little." Doctor Serocold had never
heard a word of all this before. "But she's got over
it," mused Emily, staring out of the window at a
sky turning yellow for a watery sunset, and playing
with a twisted, tasselled rope of small seed pearls.
"Girls do. . . . She had a much easier time with
the second child, and Gilbert is really very kind,
though he's not particularly amusing. I think she's
going to be sensible like the rest of us, Luke." She
turned back to Doctor Serocold with an uncertain
smile which frightened him. "Emily, what's the
matter?" he exclaimed. It was years since she had
used his name in just that tone.

She continued to smile remotely as she said,
"Well, they'll have to stand on their own feet now.
I can't go on looking after them for ever." The words
were light, but the manner was not.

"Do you mean that there's something the matter . . . with you?" he stammered in a distracted voice that had, at any rate, the merit of catching her wandering attention. "You're not being very professional to-day, Luke, dear"; she teased him with some of her old mockery. "You've got to decide whether there's anything the matter with me or not. I don't have to diagnose my own complaint. Let's have a formal . . . death-warrant."

Her hesitation before the word was extremely brief; as he continued to stare at her, with all his professional calm broken down by the look in her face, she lifted her ringed hand and laid it with a gentle and confiding touch upon her right breast. "I don't need you, really, to tell me what I've got," she said to him. "I've been pretty sure about it for some time."

He stammered, horrified. "You can't mean what you're saying. Let me look. It's probably something quite innocent. Women are always getting *that* idea for nothing." He was far more affected than she, though he struggled to hide it: she could even smile faintly at him as she said, "I'm not the imaginative kind." He knew as well as anyone that she had never indulged in fancies about her health. Her hand was

perfectly steady as she began to unfasten what seemed
an interminable row of loops and buttons down the
front of the claret-coloured dress: he watched her
miserably. "I won't call in old Mary, if you don't
mind," she said carelessly. "I'd rather not be talked
over in the village . . . yet."

His hand was much less certain as it moved in the
prescribed manner over the small, irregular, resistant
mass beneath the pucker on the skin, which had
really told him everything at the first glance. He
hardly needed to slip his fingers up to the hard
glands of the armpit before groaning, "Why didn't
you tell me sooner?"

Her colour had not changed, or else he had never
guessed before that the two delicate flecks of it stain-
ing her cheek bones were an artistic admission of her
lost youth. She laughed her short, mirthless, metallic
laugh, the harshest thing about her, and said, "Don't
we all put off telling till it's too late? Female ostriches,
with our heads in the sand, that's what we are—
afraid to look at what's coming after us."

He stared at her and said in wonder, "But you're
not that sort, Emily?" Apparently he amused her,
as he had often done unconsciously in the past, for
she laughed again and said, "We're all the same."

He protested, "But you must have guessed; you said you did. You must have known that time was everything."

"Oh, time!..." echoed she with a strange disdain. "What do I want with time nowadays?"

On that speech he gave up his reproaches and stood staring at her as if he had never seen her before. She took up her explanation in a perfectly simple and detached voice, "I had an idea that something was coming a month before Margery's baby was born. I felt the pain beginning then, but I wasn't going to say anything to you. If I had you'd have wanted me to be operated upon at once, and if I'd refused you'd have gone off and told Bill and Margery to persuade me. I wasn't going to have her upset just then for anything. I made up my mind to wait until she was all right and about again." She cocked her head at him with a queer, defiant satisfaction.

He could find nothing to say except, "It must be operated on, now, at once, and we must get radium to it afterward." To himself he said, "But I'm pretty sure I'm too late. It'll only come back again somewhere else if that heart of hers stands the operation." He had warned her some months earlier that her heart was not as strong as it had been, and he guessed that she remembered it from the tone in which she mocked him with, "Oh, you can operate now, Luke, and be damned!"

He protested, "Emily . . . Emily . . . did you want to kill yourself?" and she retorted, showing emotion for the first time in her shaking hands, as she played with the seed-pearl tassels, "Well, what have I got to live on for? Tom's dead . . . Elizabeth's gone . . . Margery doesn't need me any longer. I've done my job and I'm tired. . . . My God, I'm tired! . . ." It came over him, with a pang like a sword, that he had never heard her say just that before in all her hard-worked life.

"Can't you understand," she demanded with a failing voice, "that I may have had enough of it?" And she lay back in her armchair, which suddenly seemed to have grown a little too big for her.

"I've never been able to rest," said she, settling her head against the faded green *petit-point* embroidery of the cushion with a kind of defiance. "I've always had to keep going. There's never been quite enough time, or quite enough help, or quite enough money for the things I wanted, unless I went out to look for them myself. Tom did what he could, but he was so stupid, poor darling. I daren't trust anything important to him, for fear he'd muddle it. You knew that perfectly well, and I can admit it now, though I never would in the old days. The girls did their best to help after they grew up, but of course they had to see to their own affairs. I didn't intend to let my worries interfere with their lives. No, I've had to depend on myself all through when it came down to bedrock. I've had my job to do and I've done it; but can't you see that I shall be glad when it's over?"

Doctor Serocold looked at her and thought that, in the country phrase, there was death in her face. He dared not insult her with reassurances while her bright dark eyes admitted the secret of her exhaustion. "I don't care what you do now," she said with a terrible calm. "You can mess me about at the hospital, if you like. I shall get another year that way, perhaps, if I come through; and that'll be long enough for Elizabeth to come back, if she wants to. It's time she brought those two children home again; and I might keep her in England for a bit, while I lasted. But I don't suppose my heart will stand a great deal nowadays, thank goodness!"

He lied to that, steadily, but he did not think that she believed him. "Easier, perhaps, if she doesn't get over the shock of the operation," he thought.

"The money's all pretty straight now," she told him, as if she was turning to a more important matter. "I've been going into everything these last few weeks. I settled as much as I could spare on the girls when they married to save death duties, and Tom's money all goes to them in any case. And I've got an offer waiting for this place. I've settled the details and I shall close with it before I go into hospital. Then, whatever happens, the girls won't have anything to worry about. I can plant myself on Margery for a bit, if necessary, and you'll find me somewhere where they'll finish me off. I'm not going to have Margery nursing my last stages." Her voice had changed and strengthened again as she began to consider her plans. Doctor Serocold had seen the same thing happen a hundred times when any difficulty threatened her; and he made an old protest, "Why do you always think of everyone but yourself?"

She turned her delicate head and smiled at him. "I *am* thinking of myself," she maintained. "I like to get everything finished up comfortably and feel that my job's done. Not so badly, is it, either, Luke?" She spoke with an innocent and youthful pride. "I had been rather efficient, haven't I?" she demanded. "I may say it now?"

He groaned, "You've been the best wife . . . the best mother . . . the best friend. . . ." He could not look at her any longer, and did not see her pity; but he heard the bitter-sweet affection in her voice as she murmured, "Ah, you always thought better of me than I deserved! But then, you were in love with me . . . once upon a time."

That did make him look at her, but he did not understand immediately all that he saw. "You never guessed I knew," she teased him. "Thought you were keeping it all to yourself. Poor old thing!" It was the phrase and accent that she had had for her children in the old days when they were hurt, a laughing gentleness that forbade tears. He dared not touch her hand as he stammered, "You knew——"

"Of course I knew," triumphed she. "Where would my eyes have been to miss it? Besides, I was looking. You see, I was a little in love with you myself."

He could not choose but believe her, for the mockery was all gone from her eyes and voice, but he could only repeat with the same sense of helpless despair. "Why didn't you tell me sooner?"

"How could I?" said she, as simply as a child. "Tom was alive then and he couldn't have done without me any more than the children could. You were all right by yourself, but they were all three just about as helpless as each other when it came to looking after themselves. Besides, where would you have

been if I'd let anything come of it? A doctor who'd
got himself into a mess with the wife of one of his
patients. It's an old story, but it's never a pretty one.
We couldn't have kept it dark in a gossiping place
like this. You'd have been done for. I wasn't going
to let that happen. I just put you off. Don't you
remember that summer?"

He nodded silently, for he did remember it. "I
just made everything impossible for you for two or
three months," said she placidly. "I wouldn't let
you see anything in me except what you disliked and
despised. There was always enough of that, goodness knows: you're a much more decent person than
I am. I made you think that you were mistaken
about me. It wasn't really very difficult, after I'd
made up my mind to it. There was always someone
else that I could flirt with in front of you when you
were about, or I could make fun of you in one of the
ways you hated. You soon pulled yourself together
and decided that it was a mistake to see so much of
me. And then the war began and I was all right.
Everything was upset and you were too busy to come
near me, and I had Tom's affairs to look after. If
anything had happened to him in France," mused
Emily, still with the same staggering frankness, "I
suppose things might have been different. But he

came back again just as devoted as ever, and you'd got over it by that time, and I had to get over it too. And after he was killed it was all too late. A fire won't burn for ever if you don't mend it, you know. It's all an old story now. I never think of it and I'm certain you never think of it either. I've only gone back to it to-day because it doesn't matter any longer to either of us. But I didn't see why I should . . . die . . . without telling you." Her lips hardly seemed to tremble over the word which set her apart from him for ever.

He burst out, "It would have made all the difference to me if I had known."

"Ah, but I wouldn't let you know!" she triumphed. "If I had, everything would have been spoiled. I had my job to do and nobody else in the world could do it quite so well. And you had your job to do, and I made up my mind that you should do it properly. I counted on you for that. When I was sick of everything," said Emily, more to herself than to him, "I used to remind myself, 'There's Luke working away all alone. He doesn't much like what he's doing, and he won't ever make much out of it, and I expect he gets pretty tired of it at times. But he never gives in and I won't either.'"

She laid her hand on his and it trembled with a

strange exaltation. "I've almost finished my work now," she said. "And perhaps it hasn't amounted to very much. But, at any rate, I can look back and say I did my best with it. When you get to where I am, Luke, you'll be able to say the same."

He thought, "I'm there now, perhaps . . . to-night I shall know. Have I done my best, or has my best been worth doing? At any rate, she's braver than I am. She doesn't know how I felt this morning . . . dissatisfied . . . discouraged . . . tired out. She shan't ever know. . . . I'll go on sticking to my job till I drop, as she's done." And he gathered himself together to tell her something of what she had once meant to him, and the little that she would hear of his pity for her now. She lay back in her great chair, listening to him with her absent smile; he thought that some of his stammered words comforted her. She was much quieter than he was; she allowed him to make plans for her and agreed to carry out his orders, though he realized that she did it with the indifference of resignation to a fate which he hardly hoped to alter. One service he did promise her: "You might go to Margery's to-night and tell her what's the matter, will you?" she asked him. "Then I shan't have to. Bill's a sensible fellow; you can leave her to him."

He agreed and she drove him away with all her old, amused determination. "I've got a hundred things to do," she mocked him from the door of the stable yard, to which she had led him, protesting. "And you've got all the rest of your visits to pay, and you know Lady Catterick hates to be kept waiting."

"Oh, I'm late for her already," said the doctor crossly, as he got into his car.

"That's one to me," said Emily with satisfaction. "How I do hate that woman! But I could always keep you away from her, even in the old days, couldn't I?" She had followed him to the car and stood with her thin, ringed hand on the door of it, her dangling seed-pearl earrings shook with her mischievous laughter. He remembered the old days with a sudden terrible clearness as he looked at her, and he saw that she remembered them too, for she took a step nearer to him, and asked him abruptly, under her breath, "Luke, you'll give me plenty of morphia, won't you? It'll be all you'll be able to do for me."

He said, "I'll do everything for you, Emily. I promise," and had her hand again for a moment, while he gave her his unconvincing reassurances: he did not realize until after he had driven away

how strong the grip of her agonized fingers had been.
His hand was sore from it for half an hour of driving,
but not so sore as his heart.

III

HE DROVE through Holt Regis village and took
the Carfax turning; then ran for half a mile in the
shelter of a high brick wall, over a road whose tarred
surface was slippery with fallen golden leaves from
the double row of beeches overhead. Then he turned
in at a pair of wrought-iron gates which stood open
on an avenue of lime trees, and drove up to the house,
crossing the river Dodder once on his way by a formal
stone bridge ornamented with balls and urns, and
passing it again on his left, where it had been dammed
up into a mournful sheet of water, choked with lily
leaves and shuddering brown rushes, incapable of
reflecting the evening sky, and tenanted by a solitary
swan.

Carfax was a square and solid Palladian house,
set about with wide lawns and terraces, classical
cedars, elaborately patterned flower beds edged with
box, and a noble and sullen circle of beech woods.

The doctor left his car, looking smaller and shabbier than usual, at the foot of the lead Mercury, which poised on one toe in a waste of gravel outside the massive portico, and climbed the steps to the entrance a little wearily, hoping that fat Lady Catterick would not expect a long visit, or would, at any rate, console him with tea during its course. It was after five, and the sun was just setting in a bank of heavy cloud; there was a line of primrose colour behind the woods and a pale, melancholy light upon the tall pillars of the house; its westward-facing windows gleamed like steel. The doctor yawned and shivered a little as he waited, musing, "It looks like a wet day to-morrow. This fine weather can't last much longer. Saint Luke's summer will soon be over." And then he thought, as he always did when he came to Carfax, "It seems only the other day that this place was a hospital. A row of deck chairs there used to be all along this portico, and convalescents sunning themselves, or trying their crutches up and down the terrace when I came." The vision was quite clear for a moment and very real; it even persisted after he had been admitted; and as he crossed the immense hall, with its spiral staircase, frescoed ceiling, echoing marble flagstones and looming statues, he seemed to himself to be walking in authority between rows

of narrow beds, each with its ghostly occupant. He
blinked a little when he was ushered into the small
boudoir which had then been the commandant's
office; but Lady Catterick was not there, though
the room was brightly lit, as if she had only just left
it. Before she returned he had time to accustom his
fatigued eyes to the glitter from the crystal chandelier, repeated in her many mirrors, the sparkle of the
firelight among the polished steel and Dresden china
decorations of her white marble mantelpiece, the
glinting reflections from her bright glazed chintz
and satinwood furniture. There was an overpowering
scent of Roman hyacinths, unclosing in the warmth
of the room, which in some way confused and distracted his attention. She caught him unprepared as
he stood on her white fur hearthrug, facing her Alice-
through-the-looking-glass mantelpiece, where the
gilt clock under its protecting shade, the paired alabaster ornaments and Bohemian vases stood reflecting their backs in the mirror. He was chafing his
stiff, cold hands together busily, in a rather patheti-
cally unsuccessful imitation of the professional brisk-
ness of his youth; actually he was feeling old and
tired. He had forgotten, as he always did, the concealed door in the corner, with the green-and-white
striped satin paper continuing over it, and the clatter-

ing couple of gold-frame water colours swinging from their triangular wires on its back. The old woman came pouncing through it while his back was turned, and had the advantage of him, as she liked to have it over her visitors; she made him jump with the yapping of her savage little Pekinese dog and her sudden, loud, amused, almost contemptuous greeting, "Well, Doctor, here you are," in a tone which seemed to mean, "Here you are at last. Why didn't you get here sooner?"

She was a loud-voiced, jolly, hard, bullying person, as Victorian as her room, in many ways more like a man than a woman; tactless, heavy-handed, and fond of authority, but incapable of exercising it without falling into a series of foolish mistakes. She could not bear to take advice, and ran contrary to it with a vigour which involved her in endless difficulties; she quarrelled with anyone who opposed her, despised anyone who gave way to her, had as many enemies as any woman in the county, and could only be handled by the few people who were able to treat her with amused disregard. Doctor Serocold could get as much out of her as anyone, but he always found her extremely fatiguing, and liked to feel perfectly fresh before embarking on an encounter with her; this afternoon he was not sure that he felt quite up to her.

She had been the rich and childless widow of a North-country manufacturer, and she had married, rather late in life, Sir Philip Catterick, the last of a poor, proud, obscure county family. Doctor Serocold remembered him as a scholarly, sensitive, ineffective man, of poor health and insignificant attainments, not mentally remarkable in any way, and easily dominated by his overbearing wife. She had been attracted by his title and his house, whose gloomy solemnity had impressed her; but she had early taken his measure and decided that he would give her very little trouble. Certainly he did not do so; in fact, she must have found him an almost depressingly manageable contrast to her first husband, a noisy, bullying person with whom she had carried on an invigoratingly quarrelsome existence. She treated Sir Philip by the same methods from force of habit and was surprised to find that they reduced him to an uneasy silence. He wandered unhappily about Carfax for some years, apparently bewildered by his own position, and then died quietly one winter of a neglected cold on the chest, leaving his wife to bring up their only child. It had always been supposed that he had married her for her money, since she seemed to have no other attractions, but after his death it appeared that she had kept her fortune in her own hands, or rather that her first husband had secured it to her. Young Harry inherited merely the white elephant of a house, and his father's small income, which was insufficient of itself to maintain Carfax. However, during his minority his mother managed the affairs of the estate, spent a good deal of her own money, not altogether wisely, upon it, and greatly enjoyed the exercise of a dowager's authority. She was a short, stout, high-coloured, hard-featured woman; her face belonged to what Doctor Serocold privately called the bloodhound type; she had a sagging, heavy jowl, and cheeks empurpled with distended capillaries; the patronizing arch of her bushy eyebrows corresponded to the downward dragging corners of a small, compressed, and obstinate mouth. She spoke in an authoritative, aggressive voice, and bit off her words as if she enjoyed the taste of them. Standing or moving she was a thick, ungraceful figure, short in the legs and with immense, clumsy hips and shoulders; but when she was sitting, as now, behind her tea table, fenced in by its silver and china, staring at the doctor with a baleful glitter of her eyeglasses and squaring her broad bust at him, there was something formidable about her commonplace ugliness.

He sat uncomfortably in one of her slippery chintz-covered chairs, feeling the fire scorch one side of his face and body, listening in an absent-minded fashion to her booming account of her own health and scalding his mouth with a cup of her bitter Indian tea, while he made assenting noises, saved his energies for the discussion about her son which he intended to provoke later, and thought, "You old hag, I wish you had anything really the matter with you! If you've brought me out all this way just to talk about your own symptoms, I could have saved myself the drive. I can tell you exactly what they are myself, but I can't do anything for them as long as you go on stuffing yourself up with masses of food four times a day and never taking any exercise except when you get pottering up and down the terrace with that confounded yapping dog of yours and nibbling chocolate creams whenever you've a minute to fill in. There's a two-pound box of them, half-empty, with the lid off, behind you now on the card table. No wonder you're the size you are!" He disliked Lady Catterick as much as anyone in his practice. Her only merit was she paid full fees and did not keep him waiting for his money.

She was jabbering on, "And you know, I never can stand an east wind. As soon as I wake up in the morning I can tell if there's an east wind. It puts me in a bad temper for the day." He thought, "I wonder what you're like when you're in a good one. I've never seen the spectacle, as far as I can remember," and rejected his second cup with disgust. It was as bitter as ink. "And just about as digestible, for me," he reflected with apprehension. But a doctor has little time to think of his own symptoms. He pushed his chair back from the fire, repeated some old advice which he knew would be disregarded, jotted down a new prescription, recommended a diet, and concluded, "I think perhaps it's time you did another three weeks at Bath, Lady Catterick. Bath always does you good." And he added in his own mind, "I dare say Harry will be glad enough to be rid of you for a little, if all I hear is true. Bath's a long way off, if I can persuade you to go there alone."

She interrupted his meditations with a kind of snort, a very piglike noise which made him think of an old sow wallowing in a mud heap. "I dare say it *would* do me good, Doctor Serocold, but I can't afford to consider myself at present. It's my duty to stop here and look after Harry."

Doctor Serocold groaned under his breath and

inquired, "How is Sir Harry? I haven't seen the boy lately." For this was in point of fact the errand that he had come upon.

"Oh, Harry gets no better," declared his mother impatiently, while the doctor wondered, "Is that one of your lies, or don't you really know?" "He's not at all well just now," said Lady Catterick, "and he's being extremely annoying."

"It would annoy you, of course, if he really wants to get married," reflected Doctor Serocold, as she continued to grumble vaguely. "You might get turned out at last. You've had a long run for your money. Harry was only ten when his father died, and you were able to bring him up entirely under your own thumb, and manage the estate just as you liked, and get things into as much of a muddle as the solicitors would stand. Luckily the boy's own money was tied up, such as it was; he'd always have enough to live on quietly if he sold the place. But when he grew up you stuck on and kept matters in your own hands as much as you could. You never let Harry develop any will of his own and you always rubbed it in to him that he couldn't afford to live here if it weren't for your help. You took pretty good care that he never learned any other way of supporting himself except sponging on you, and he

came to depend on you for everything. I know he
went to the war and I know he got pretty badly
smashed up; it's the only thing there is to be said
for him, so far. You did your best to keep him at
home as long as you could, but it wasn't from affection, I'm certain, however much you talked about
widows' sons. You simply didn't want him to get
away from your apron strings. Of course, you made
a lot of fuss over him when he did go, and managed
to sound very patriotic about it, just as you managed
to make quite an impressive spectacle of turning
Carfax into an officers' hospital, and ploughing up
some corner of the park that you couldn't see from
your windows to grow a few potatoes in. But you
were clever enough to see that you got your money's
worth out of being commandant, and sailing about
in that white uniform that you invented for yourself,
and interfering with people like Ellen Archibald,
who did your work for you, and bullying a lot of
girls who were frightened by the noise you made,
and having yourself photographed for the papers
with a group of your patients on the front steps. You
still enjoy boasting about it all, and telling people
how useful you were, but I remember the muddles
you made and the rows you got up with the authorities, and the way you would have spoiled the whole

thing if you could. No thanks to you if the place wasn't shut up in six months. It was the rest of us who had to pull it through."

And as she continued to tell him things that he had already heard and did not believe about her son's health, he thought, "Of course, the boy isn't like anyone else. You needn't tell me that. I've got the X-ray plates of his skull at home in the surgery. I know where the bullet went. But he's not had one of those fits for six years. They were simply due to the splinter of bone that was pressing on the brain, and they stopped as soon as that was relieved by the operation. No earthly reason for them ever to recur. And he told me as long ago as last winter that he'd stopped dreaming about the trenches. If he's started that again you know as well as I do whose fault it must be. Of course he's a bit of a neurasthenic, but what else can you expect if you spend all your time suggesting that he can't work because of his eyesight, and that he'll have to avoid excitement for the rest of his life for fear of bringing on one of his headaches? If you've been storming and raging at him about this new idea of his, I don't wonder he's worse. However, I've only your word for that." And he asked whether Sir Harry wished to see him professionally.

"I don't know whether he does or not," said Lady Catterick in her own offensive fashion. "But I particularly told him that he must come in early. *I* wish you to see him." She spoke as if her son were ten years old instead of having reached the twenty or thirty with which the doctor's hasty calculations credited him. "I want you to give him a good talking to about his health."

"Oh, you do, do you?" thought the doctor rebelliously. "I suppose he won't listen to you." And he remarked that he did not suppose there was any reason to alter the young man's régime.

Lady Catterick snorted, "Oh, Harry gets on all right as long as he keeps quiet. It's all this new nonsense." She choked over her indiscretion, almost dropped her teacup, and then spluttered and coughed into her handkerchief for some time in a disgusting fashion which was peculiar to her. Doctor Serocold waited grimly until this paroxysm subsided, noting how dangerously it deepened her apoplectic colour; and then inquired, "What new nonsense?" though he knew perfectly well what she was talking about.

Finding herself obliged to come to the point, she did so with vigour. "He's taken it into his head that he wants to marry the parson's daughter at Holt Abbas," she exploded. "Absolute nonsense!"

"Angela Fletcher?" murmured the doctor, who had known the girl all her life.

"Angela, or Pamela, or Diana, or some such affected nonsense," said Lady Catterick, who presumably knew the name as well as he did. "The one who went off to London in that ridiculous way to earn her own living. In my day she'd have stayed at home and kept quiet and helped her father in the parish. But I suppose she wanted the money. They're all as poor as church mice. I hear she was in church last Sunday in clothes that were most unsuitable for the country. I don't suppose her father paid for them."

"I hear she's got quite a good job, drawing fashions for some paper," observed the doctor with satisfaction.

"Illustrations for ridiculous articles—young women in pajamas on the Lido, and so forth," snapped Lady Catterick, who had apparently seen them. "Legs two yards long and no figures to speak of. I see nothing beautiful in them. In my time you could tell the young men from the young women, but apparently that's out of date. She won't be able to keep Harry and herself out of a page of drawings a week."

"She won't have to," objected the doctor, beginning to lose his temper. "He's got some money of his own, after all."

"Oh, enough to live in some wretched flat in Earl's Court, I dare say. That's what they talk of doing. He'd find it a bit of a change from Carfax."

"Got as far as that, have they? Promising!" thought the doctor, and aloud he protested, "Come, Lady Catterick, not as bad as that. They could be perfectly comfortable together in a quiet way without your having to give them a penny."

"I certainly shouldn't help them." He believed her this time without difficulty, and it pleased him to observe her annoyance when he retorted, "Of course, Harry could always sell this place."

She spluttered over that. "Sell Carfax? How can you say such a thing? Why, it's the family place: the Cattericks have lived here always. Harry may be the last of them, but he'd have better feeling than to give up the house." She did not sound as if she were convincing herself, and Doctor Serocold thought, "A lot of rubbish! You may pretend to care about the house, but the boy doesn't. He's bored to death with it—has been for years—and it's your fault for the way you've stuffed it down his throat. His father would have given him a different set of ideas if he'd lived. All Harry wants now is to get away." And he said aloud, "I shouldn't wonder if Harry were to fancy London, for a change."

Lady Catterick burst out spitefully, "You won't find the girl does. Depend upon it, that's all a blind. What she wants is to turn me out and take my place here. That's what she's been working for all along. But she'll not find it so easy."

"I don't believe Angela expects anything of the kind," declared the doctor, getting angry in his turn.

The old woman interrupted him with, "Of course she does. Of course she does. What else has she been running after Harry all this time for? You don't imagine she's in love with him, do you?" as he made some sort of interruption. "How could she be? How could any girl be? Why, the boy's blind!"

IV

SHE was screeching so loudly that she did not hear the door open behind her. It was Doctor Sero-cold who saw it move and shouted her down with, "You don't know what you're talking about." He hoped that he would prevent her son from hearing what she was saying. The young man had heard, however: that was obvious from the dazed manner in which he advanced across the floor, cautiously feeling his way with his stick among the insecure little chairs and tables with which it was encumbered. There was no particular change in the expression of his face, but then he had only half of it with which to express his feelings. The other half had been composed by the surgeons into a deceptively human brown mask, with a scar or two now faded into insignificance about the empty orbit. There was no eye on this side: the remaining eye seemed to move in response to its surroundings, but it was dull and glazed; it perceived little more than the difference between light and darkness. The untouched side of the face was handsome enough: there was little need, in any but the strongest light, for a nervous trick which the young man had developed of putting up one hand to his injured cheekbone, as if he wanted to hide what had been done for him by the surgeons. Doctor Serocold would have described Harry's face as a good cosmetic result. As for what lay behind it, he considered that, professionally speaking, a good result also: but he was a little anxious about how much it would be able to stand in the next half-hour or so. He was thankful to find that astonishment and annoyance had silenced Lady Catterick for the moment. In the dreadful pause that followed he was able to say something quieting to the young man and to steady him a little by grasping his hand. It felt cold and damp, as usual, but it was firm in its response. The uncertain head turned toward him; the dim single eye appeared to move in an effort to perceive him, though its owner was incapable of finding anything to say to him before the old woman returned to her attack. "So you've come back, Harry, I told Doctor Serocold I wanted him to see you." She spoke as if the matter were already arranged.

Her Indian tea, however, bad as it had been, had revived the doctor's failing energies to the point of giving battle. "You don't look as if you wanted a consultation," said he, in a cheerful and aggressive tone, turning his shoulder upon her.

"No more I do," responded Harry Catterick ungraciously, with a quiver of the active side of his face. His voice, heard thus for the first time, had a muffled, disused quality: his words came in jerks, as if he had to force them out of himself. He moved his head nervously from side to side, as if he were trying to make out where his mother and the doctor were sitting.

"Don't talk such nonsense," rapped out the old woman. "Of course you must see Doctor Serocold.

If you won't listen to me, you must listen to him. He'll tell you how impossible it is for you to think of getting married."

There was the same faint movement of the living side of Harry's face, but this time he did not manage to drive any words between his teeth. He took a step backward, as if he wanted to get away from his mother's voice; and then something else made him hold his ground. He stood sullenly, clenching his hands at his sides and twisting his head a little toward his left shoulder: it was a defensive trick he had as if he were trying to get a fair field of vision for the dim eye which remained. The sight of him thus handicapped made Doctor Serocold break out abruptly and savagely, "I shan't tell him anything of the kind. Let him get married if he likes."

The words fell like stones into an amazed silence; the doctor, as much disturbed by them as anyone, continued furiously, "The best thing in the world for him, if Angela is mad enough to do it. Let her take him right away from here and give him a peaceful life. It's what he's always wanted and never had. I know the girl: she's quiet and steady and strong: she'll mother him, if you won't. She's the sort of person to cure him. How is he ever to get any control of himself as long as he's badgered and bullied and shouted at? If he takes my advice, he'll go up to London to-morrow with her and get a special license."

In the appalled hush that followed his words he heard the old woman gasping and snorting to get her breath, and had time to think to himself, "Well, I shan't ever have to drive out here again on her account now, whatever happens." The thought gave him a certain gloomy satisfaction. He had always thought visits to Lady Catterick a hard way of earning money.

Harry was staring at him with confusion, even with alarm; he looked as if the doctor's words had thoroughly frightened him. The old woman began to splutter and struggle apoplectically, clutching at the arms of her chair and trying to lift herself up: but between her bulk and the shortness of her breath she was obliged to remain where she was, heaving and blowing, and gradually getting words together for a storm of abuse. Doctor Serocold judged it best to let her get this over: it was violent enough when it came, but fortunately it was mainly directed toward himself. He thought, "This runs off me like water off a duck's back. So long as she doesn't start on the boy, I don't care what she says to me. She can tire herself out that way and welcome. He's not standing it too badly."

He kept the tail of his eye on Harry, who had got his back against the door by this time; he was apparently keeping his nerves under control, with only the lop-sided frown on his forehead and the twist of his bitten lip to show how he winced from the harsh sound of his mother's voice, which filled the hot, bright, scented little room with clamour. "But his head must be feeling as if it were splitting in half by now," reflected the doctor. He decided, too late, that it was time to stop the old woman's ravings, just as she tired of him and rounded on her son with, "I don't know what Doctor Serocold is thinking about, to talk as he does. What right has anyone in your state to marry? What sort of a husband do you expect to make? What kind of children are you going to have?"

The unfortunate young man put both hands to his ears, as if he could not bear to listen any longer, and Doctor Serocold got to his feet with clumsy haste. He took the dumb and distracted young man by the arm and told him urgently, "Don't listen to another word. Come away with me; it's your only chance. If you stop here you'll be finished . . . argued over . . . shouted down. You'll never be able to stand it. You haven't the strength. The only thing for you to do is to clear out."

The young man said nothing, but Doctor Serocold heard him give a faint, despairing groan: he was past speech, but not too dazed to move. Doctor Serocold took him by the elbows as if he were drunk, and fairly ran him out of the room, leaving the old woman gobbling and swearing. The next thing that he remembered was descending the steps outside with Harry, and the cold evening air blowing about them and a small star pricking the green sky above the overhanging cornice of the roof. The newly alighted Mercury seemed to point to it with his hand as the doctor demanded, "Is Angela at Holt Abbas, at her father's house? Can you go to her?"

Harry murmured, "yes . . . yes . . ." and as the doctor pushed him into the waiting car and started the engine, he thought, "This is a pretty extraordinary proceeding on my part. Simple melodrama and no business of mine . . . kidnapping, you might call it. I wonder what on earth made me do it! I must be out of my mind." Yet he had no doubt at all that what he was doing was justified; and as they drove down the avenue, where the lights of the car made a white tunnel between the bleached stems of the beeches, he thought, "I swear the boy'll be all right as soon as he gets to his Angela."

Holt Abbas was not more than two miles away,

though it was a little out of the doctor's road. Not
many minutes after they had left the park the headlights of the car shone upon the first houses of the
village; and after he had passed the crossroads and
the church they turned in at the vicarage gate. Half-
way up the drive, however, the young man, who
had been sitting in a lump beside the doctor and
giving no sign of life, suddenly moved, clutched him
by the arm and cried out, "Stop!"

The doctor, with an oath, saved the steering wheel
from the hands upon it and pulled up the car with
its nose in a laurel bush, whose glittering leaves
pushed up against the wind screen. "What the devil
did you grab at me like that for?" he demanded.
"Why don't you think what you're doing?"

Harry was muttering something that he could not
hear: he had to switch off the engine before he made
out, "Was she right?"

"Was who right? Oh, your mother! . . . Good
God!" exploded the doctor. "Have I got to go
into all that here—in the middle of a laurel bush?"
He wanted, suddenly and savagely, to finish the
whole business and get home. Harry's affairs were too
fantastic at the end of a long day, and he was too
tired to argue. "No . . . no . . . no . . ." he insisted furiously. "There's nothing wrong with you now, except

what your mother makes you fancy. What you want is a year away from her, in a new place, with Angela to look after you. She can't cure your eyes, but she can cure your mind. It'll be hell for her, I should say, but it's her own choice: I've talked it over with her already. . . . She knows what's best for you. Are you going to spend the rest of your life loafing round after that old woman?" He thought, with a flash of compunction, "What right have I to talk to the boy like this? It's not his fault that he's been allowed to get into such a state. But I've got to cure him somehow." And he said, as if he were in a rage, "It's your last chance."

He thought that he had been too savage when he saw the young man's face, as white as death and seeming to stare at him as if he had suddenly become visible; then he told himself that it was only the ghastly glare of the headlights which made Harry look so strange. "Look here, my boy," he began, forcing himself to patience and deliberation, "you were pretty bad when you came back from France. Your skull was all smashed up; and after the first wound healed, and you were discharged from the army, there was still that splinter of bone from the inner table of the skull pressing on your brain and making you have those queer fits of yours. I spotted

that and got you up to London for your operation.
It was perfectly successful; but you couldn't hope
to recover in a month or so, for all that. Naturally
you still had your headaches, and your bad dreams,
and your neurasthenic ways. I didn't expect you to
pull yourself together immediately, or start managing
your own affairs. If you'd been a poor man you'd
have had to do it; but you were fairly well off and
thoroughly spoiled, and you had a mother who'd
brought you up to be entirely dependent on her. I
made allowances for you. I gave you a year or two
to find your feet, but you haven't done it. You've
gone on slacking about, letting your mother do what
she liked with the place and you, and thinking yourself a hopeless wreck, long after there was any need
for it. I was beginning to be afraid that you would
let yourself slide for the rest of your life. When I
heard you were playing about with Angela I was
annoyed at first; I'd known her all her life, and
frankly, I thought she was too good to be wasted
on you. But afterward she made me see that she
was your only chance. If she would take you on there
might be some hope for you. I went to see your
mother on purpose, to find out how she was taking
it all. When I saw what her position was, I determined to make you do something definite. Now I

wash my hands of you. I've brought you here, and you can decide for yourself whether you're going into the house or whether I'm to turn right round and drive you back home." He completed this lecture in a laurel bush by putting the car into reverse and twisting it back on to the drive.

"But if she—if Angela—if she's unhappy——" Harry began to stammer.

"She's old enough to know what she wants," said the doctor crossly. "But you can ask her yourself in a minute what she feels about it. I'm not going to sit here any longer." And he decided that after all he would have to settle the matter himself. With an impatience which gave no hint of the pity beneath it, he started the car again and drove up to the vicarage porch.

The oaken, nail-studded door was gaping wide as usual, country-fashion: and the doctor was too familiar with the Fletchers' circumstances to expect a servant to answer the bell. He got out of the car, strode up the steps and into the dim shadows of the hall; glanced sharply about him and discovered, beyond the circle of illumination from the one oil lamp half-way up the stairs, between the varnished Gothic banisters like pew-ends and the case of stuffed humming-birds at the turn of the landing, a movement which justified his calling up, "Here, you, Midge, what are you doing there?"

The moving object revealed itself as a small, sharp-featured girl of ten or eleven, in a much-mended blue jersey and skirt, with a struggling terrier of uncertain breeding in her arms. She descended the stairs reluctantly and retorted, "What are you doing yourself? Is anyone hurt?"

"Not this time," replied the doctor, who was used to the family chapter of accidents. "Where *is* everybody?"

"I thought it might be one of the boys," explained Miss Fletcher in a disappointed tone, coming down another step. "Father's in church, of course. Mother's in the kitchen, talking to cook about the blackberry jam. Angela's upstairs. Philly's shutting up the chickens. John's cleaning his bicycle, and Mary's practising in the drawing room." She detailed this information in a singsong, matter-of-fact tone, as monotonous as the five-finger exercises which confirmed her last item from behind the varnished pitch-pine door of the drawing room. She took a fresh hold on the dog, which was covering her with white hairs in its efforts to escape: and then stared at Harry Catterick, who at that moment appeared uncertainly in the doorway. "What's the matter with *him?*" she inquired with interest. "He looks as if he'd taken a toss."

"You get along out of here," replied the doctor, without enlightening her. "And tell Angela I want her in the schoolroom."

"All right," agreed Midge, with the placid obedience of the youngest in a large family. "But you might tell me what's up." And as she retraced her steps upstairs she leaned over the moth-eaten bearskin rug that hung from the landing to volunteer the information, "Angela won't like being disturbed. She's packing to go to London."

"The devil she is," thought the doctor. "I'm just in time."

He was perfectly accustomed to the Fletchers' schoolroom, with its rows of battered books and ink-stained tablecloth, its nursery relics of doll's house, rocking horse, and Walter Crane wall paper, never renewed, its litter of carpentering tools and shavings, wireless apparatus, dressmaking pins and patterns, tennis rackets, hockey sticks, caps, shoes, and tea things. He was surprised but thankful to find it empty: he pushed Harry into one of the torn and dusty leather armchairs, and fidgeted himself in a nervous and irritable fashion on the hearthrug, with his back to the smouldering fire of sticks and pine

cones that the children had gathered, trying stupidly
to tell the time from the intricately carved face of the
nursery cuckoo clock hanging on the opposite wall,
instead of consulting his own watch, and calculating
frenziedly, "Half-past six. Why on earth did I start
all this to-day? I shall never get home."

In the middle of his calculations the expected
noise at the door ended in the appearance of Angela
Fletcher, tall, fair, solid, and looking capable of
everything that was sensible. His heart turned over
with thankfulness when he saw her; and he said,
in a voice which betrayed the whole of his anxiety
and relief, "Here's something else that you'd better
take with you to London."

The manner in which she exclaimed "Harry!"
seemed to the doctor to justify the whole of his interference. He felt satisfied with his recent proceedings
when he saw her cross the room, drop down on the
arm of the young man's chair, and draw him to her
breast like a mother. He was entirely unconscious of
anyone but her: he turned to her and buried his face
against her shoulder, clinging to her with desperate
hands. The doctor heard him say, as if to explain
everything, "I came to you." She put her cheek down
on his hair for a moment, and then she looked up at

the doctor and asked in an undertone that did not disturb the young man's attitude, "What's happened?"

Doctor Serocold replied, after a brief hesitation and with the beginnings of amusement, "I've kidnapped him, and I advise you to do the same."

She made no sort of exclamation, merely sat looking at him above her lover's head with serious and considering eyes. "Are you going to London to-night?" inquired the doctor.

She said, "I was."

"Well, then, go, and take him with you," advised Doctor Serocold, watching her for the start that she did not give. "Don't let anyone know where you are and get married as soon as you can. He's not fit for the sort of row that he's had to go through to-night, and he'll get nothing else as long as he stays at Carfax. What he wants is you to look after him. Get married and away, and the old woman's teeth are drawn. She'll have to give in, or if she doesn't, you can keep him out of her way until he's himself again. I should recommend taking him to some cheap, quiet place abroad for six months. And don't send any of us the address." He delighted in the faint answering smile that came about her lips.

"It sounds like a good prescription," was all she said.

The doctor exploded, "Damn it all, you're both old enough to know what you're doing, and you've got enough money to please yourselves. It's not the sort of thing one advises every day, but I'm certain it's the right thing in this case. I shouldn't tell you to do it unless I were sure that you could cure him."

He spoke low and urgently, confident that the young man would not realize what he was saying. "You'll have a pretty bad time with him at first," he told her. "Just now he's too knocked about to make up his mind to anything. You'll have to take charge of him entirely. I don't need to tell you how gentle you'll have to be with him. As far as the present goes, you won't be getting a husband, you'll be getting something more like a child. You'll be taking on the most difficult job you can imagine. In the ordinary course of things I should naturally say, Wait a year: but as it is, I say, Don't wait a day longer than you can help. Take him up to London to-night, and manage the business for yourself. I promise you that it'll turn out all right in the end."

He stopped because he was frightened by the violence of his own emotion. He found the girl staring at him with a wide, fascinated look. As he watched her she closed her eyes and a long shiver went through her; then she opened them again, set her shoulders, put the young man gently away from her, and got up from her chair. "I'll do it," she said.

Harry Catterick did not seem to hear her; he sat with his elbows on his knees and his head in his hands; the girl glanced at him sideways and held out her hand to the doctor. "Leave him to me," she advised. "I'll settle everything. I was driving up to London to-night in my car. I'll take him along and fix him up somewhere and make the arrangements as soon as I can. I had an idea it might come to this, but I wanted to give his mother her chance." She spoke in amazingly collected tones, as if such things happened every day.

The doctor realized that she had taken the whole matter out of his hands, and as he listened to her further quiet suggestions he thought, "This is the modern elopement with a vengeance. She and I making plans, and the young man out of it! Her car —her money—her show altogether—it's enough to make one laugh. Topsy-turvy—I don't know whether I'm on my head or my heels! But I'm sure it'll all come right in the end." And aloud he said, "Yes,

I'll do whatever you want down here. I'll telephone
to that man of his, and send him up to-morrow with
clothes and so on; and write to you about his mother,
if she lets me get anywhere near her. But I should
think Doctor Jevons will be attending her to-morrow
—probably for an apoplectic fit. . . ."

He smiled grimly at himself and at the whole
situation. "Got enough money?" he asked Angela,
as if she were a man; and when she reassured him on
this point he said, "Well, you've no idea how late I
am already for my evening surgery. I must leave the
rest of it to you. But if there's anything more I can
do for you afterward——"

"You've done more than we shall ever forget,
already," said Angela; and the grasp of her hand
repeated what she had said. Harry Catterick was
beginning to lift his head and look about him, like
a man recovering from a heavy fall; but the doctor
could not stay for him. He left the two of them to
settle their own affairs.

As he passed through the hall he glanced up to
find out if the inquisitive Midge was still hiding
behind the banister, but he could not see her; and
he made his escape from the vicarage with a sense of
relief, thinking, "Now if the old man had come
back from church, or her mother in from the kitchen,

I should have been stuck there for the evening, trying to explain myself; and serve me right. Now they can all argue it out without me—not that Angela will let them do much arguing. She's always known what she wanted. She'll get her own way all right in the end. I'm not sure that I can quite stand up to these modern girls."

He had a passing vision of Jean Gordon, who no doubt by this time was composedly sitting beside the green-shaded lamp in the surgery, interviewing his evening patients for him, and he thought, as he rather wearily started his car, "I must be getting old. These excitements are a bit too much for me. How the old woman screamed! I should like to cut her throat. She and I are the same generation, really. I remember a bit more about my youth than she does, though; I know what those two young idiots feel about each other. Angela put her arms about him as if he were a child. She'll make a good mother, one of these days. Mustn't think of that yet, though. . . . But I'm sure the boy will be all right in the end. Not altogether sane, my behaviour. . . . Well, I'm used to making a fool of myself by this time. At any rate, I've given them their chance. They've got something to look forward to. Wish I were back where they are. . . . But I'm sixty-five . . . and I can't do my work as I used to . . . and I'm alone in the world. Catherine's dead, and Emily's dying. And no one will ever look at me again as that girl looked at Harry when she came into the room."

He got into the car and drove away.

PART V

I

W H E N he got back he found Jean Gordon sitting
at her table as he had pictured her, and watching
the clock, which pointed to ten minutes past seven.
The patients were all gone and she was leaning her
head on her hand and smoking a cigarette: it struck
him that for once she seemed a little tired. As he
sat down beside her, and glanced over the case book
which she mutely pushed toward him, he apologized
for leaving all the work to her. She roused herself at
that sufficiently to give him her faint and serious
smile, and to say, "It's all right, Doctor Serocold.
There wasn't work for two. Hardly anyone turned
up."

"I've been very much delayed," he explained. "I
was longer at the hospital than I expected, and that
made me late for Mrs. Unwin, and then I had to go
all the way out to Carfax, and back by Holt Abbas."
He did not detail to her the sum of his activities in
either house: perhaps by this time he was a little
ashamed of them: but his mind continued to dwell on
them unconsciously as he ticked off the various cases
she had seen for him, noted her treatment of them,

and closed the book. He sighed a little then, stretched himself wearily in his chair, and came out, as if it were part of a conversation between them, with the decision, "I don't think much of the young men nowadays."

His Scotch girl seemed amused by this, and turned a face that was more lively than usual toward him as she murmured, "What makes you say that?"

"Oh, something I saw this afternoon," said he, teasing her curiosity. "You'll hear all about it in good time—everyone will. . . . But seriously, now, don't you think they're rather feeble? I'm talking of one who's a bit of a left-over—don't count him. In his case there's an excuse." He knew that he need not mention a name for her to understand him. "Still, the boys I see about the town nowadays—aren't they pretty slack—not what their elder brothers were—don't they seem out to amuse themselves and dodge their work? Are you girls satisfied with what you're getting? Hasn't the war taken away the good stuff and left a lot of rubbish? Or am I just making a noise like an old man?" He found himself waiting with a real anxiety for her reply. "Aren't they rather poor stock?" he urged her.

She had a very delicate colour that came and went disarmingly and often betrayed the professional inflexibility of her voice. When she blushed she looked absurdly young, and she began blushing now, deeply and deliciously, as she burst out, with an unexpected and to him delightful candour, "I know one that isn't."

He was so surprised that he laughed outright with pleasure. "To think of her giving herself away like that, all in a minute," he said to himself. "I never caught her off her guard before. I suppose it's the end of a long day." The angry, burning colour in her cheeks, with its mixture of brown and rose, was the sweetest thing he had seen for years. "I hope he's all she thinks him," he mused, behind the smile with which he regarded her. "They're so apt not to be. But she isn't fanciful: she's shrewd. I dare say she knows a good man when she sees one." And he asked her, teasingly, "In Scotland?"

"Of course in Scotland," snapped she, beginning to master the colour in her face, and putting on her thorniest manner to cover her mistake. "I don't know anything about the men down here." She made it sound quite unnecessarily contemptuous, probably to distract his attention; but he was not to be diverted. "Haven't noticed them?" he agreed soothingly. "Had your mind elsewhere?"

She seemed at that to come to the decision that he

was not worth deceiving: she lifted her head with a quick movement which tossed back her short, fair hair, and answered coolly, "Not my mind—my heart."

He liked her all the more for it: she sounded so steady and determined. "Makes me think of that psalm we had in church lately," he reflected oddly. "*My heart is fixed, O God . . . my heart is fixed.* She won't change, either. I know her kind—like a rock. She means every word she says." And while he told her, in his fatherly way, "I'm sure your heart's in the right place, wherever it is," he began to wonder what difference all this might make to him. "Perhaps that was why she came out with it," he said to himself. "She doesn't usually give away anything unless she means to. She must be going to marry the man."

As if she had read his thoughts, or perhaps because she had planned to say something of the kind already, even if not in quite this fashion, she began to explain herself. "Donald and I are going to set up in practice together as soon as he's finished his present job. He's got another four months to do at the Royal. Then we shall look out for a place where he can get some surgery as well as the general work. He's pretty good at surgery." Doctor Serocold liked the matter-of-fact way in which she said it: evidently she was proud of her young man, but he did not think that, for all her enthusiasm, she was exaggerating. "And what are you going to do?" he inquired. "Oh, the anæsthetics, and the odd jobs, and the mothers and babies," said she cheerfully. "That's what I like." She seemed perfectly content with the second place, and apparently did not find the prospect uninteresting. "It's always useful for one doctor to marry another," she pronounced, seriously. "They can fit in with one another's work."

Doctor Serocold replied with a gravity which equalled her own, "I suppose that's why you're doing it," and she got as far as beginning in her literal fashion, "Not altogether . . ." before she glanced at him, as sharply as a robin, and found him smiling to himself. If he had wanted to see her sweet colour again he had his opportunity, but she was not offended, though she did murmur reproachfully, "It's all very well for you to laugh at us."

He said quickly, "I'm not laughing at you. I wish I were his age," and for a moment he really did.

Her Scotch habit of mind made her uncertain as to how she should take this, and she was ill at ease for a moment. He asked, to encourage her, "Have you known each other a long time?"

"All our lives," said she, forgetting him, or seeing

someone else instead of him as she smiled happily at him. He had a pang of unjustifiable resentment. "Some red-headed, bony, unimaginative lad," he told himself, "with big hands, and gloomy ways, and an accent that the people here would never follow." Nevertheless, he found himself asking, with a certain caution, "Have you decided where you're going?"

"No, we've got to look about us," said she, with an air of unconsciousness in which he could find no flaw. "We've not got too much money, either of us, though I think we could scrape together about two thousand. Still, that would hardly get us both shares in any practice. I dare say we shall just have to put up a plate in some big town and wait for patients. They say you do very well that way." He thought, "I could save you that if I chose—take you in for a thousand now, as you know the place; and let your young man come as assistant, and buy his way in gradually later, if he suits. The two of you together might solve my difficulties. You're known already, and plenty of people like you; but you're not enough for me by yourself. I must have a man for some things. If this Scotch boy of yours is as good as you think he is, allowing for a reasonable amount of prejudice on your part, he might be just what I want. I could break in the two of you gently, and turn the practice over to you in three or four years, when I really want to retire." He had got as far as that before he recollected his fears for his own health. Jean Gordon's love story had put them out of his mind for the time being, but now they kept him from making the proposal which rose to his lips. "I've only got six months, or a year, if there *is* a growth," he reminded himself. "And I haven't seen the lad. No use raising her hopes to-night for nothing." The sight that escaped him made the girl look up and ask anxiously, "What's the matter?"

"Nothing," said he untruthfully. "I'm just tired. I think I'll have a drink." And he turned toward the cupboard where he kept such things. Coming back with a rather yellow whisky-and-soda, he said, "You look a bit tired yourself, for that matter."

"I am," she admitted, unusually for her. "I've been on the go all day, and I'm not through yet. And I'm worried about that woman at Starvecrow Farm. I can't make up my mind about her symptoms. I'm beginning to think that I've made a mistake about her."

"I dare say you have," the doctor said, with a brisk irritability which he knew she would not misunderstand. And sipping his drink, he continued, "We all do, from time to time. When you get to my age, you'll only worry about the number of times you make the same mistake in a year. We learn the whole list in our hospital days—the ambulatory case of typhoid—the child with croup who's really a laryngeal diphtheria—the sprain that turns out to have been a fracture—though X-rays are killing that —the old man who seems to be drunk, and dies of a cerebral hæmorrhage. We learn them off by heart, and think they'll never puzzle us, but we get caught by them all in turn, and by a dozen more that I've forgotten to mention. If it takes three falls to make a horseman, I'm sure it takes three murders to make a doctor." He had flattered himself that he could force her to smile, and this did it. He watched her two dimples as she said, "How many have you got to your score, Doctor Serocold?"

He retorted, "Ah! You can't expect me to give that away"; and continued, quite gently for him, "If that woman at Starvecrow is what you think she is, you'll be able to do something for her. If she's the other thing, you can't cure her: you can only make her a little more comfortable. In nine cases out of ten one can't do more for people than that. You'll realize it in time. One starts out with a great notion of curing disease, but one ends by being thankful when one's able to relieve it. Ours is a patching-up job, when all's said and done. We're helpless over the big things, and they defeat us in the end." His voice had dropped heavily: he was thinking of Emily Unwin.

"You're rather—discouraging," the girl said.

He admitted, "I'm rather discouraged to-night, but it's about my own affairs, I don't want to discourage you. When you get to my time of life you'll be thankful that you've been allowed to help as often as you have. That's all I meant to say to you." And he asked her, to change the current of her thoughts, whether she had much more to do.

"Only Mrs. Perkins again after dinner," said she. "But I dare say she'll keep me up half the night."

"Everything normal?" They had both been a little worried about this particular maternity case.

"Oh, so far," said she composedly. "But it's going to be one of these endless jobs. She's been at it since last night, and she takes a lot of reassuring. I've been in and out all day. You know how it is with an elderly mother and a first child."

Doctor Serocold nodded, and said, "I'll look in on my way back from Mrs. Sinclair's, before I go to bed, if you're still there, and see whether we can hurry things up."

"I wish you would," said the Scotch girl. "She's

certain to be asking for you. They all do. They only put up with me because you can't be in two places at once."

He was flattered against his own judgment, and smiled after her as she left him to go to her lodgings in the High Street for her dinner. She had a couple of rooms over the hairdresser's shop, where she seemed to have made herself pretty comfortable, and had the advantage of being able to get her fair hair cropped by her landlord after hours.

Left to himself, Doctor Serocold made a series of notes in his day-book, drank his whisky-and-soda leisurely, and meditated upon the day's events. He did not find that he had any particular appetite for his dinner when it appeared on the table in his stuffy, uncomfortable, black leather and mahogany sitting room upstairs. Mrs. Purvis had always been an uninteresting cook; and her chief merit was her willingness to produce scratch meals at unexpected hours.

Unprompted by her master, she alternated between resistant chops or steaks and monumental pies which defied his hunger for days together. To-night seemed to be his turn for a slice of leathery beekfsteak, masked in a brown glutinous sauce, and heaped with carrot slices; he liked it even less than the waxy potatoes and mound of chopped greens accompanying it, or the solid rice pudding which followed it. However, he consumed a wary helping of each, propping up the current number of *Punch*, which he had not yet had an opportunity to read that week, against the cruet stand to help him through, but not finding it quite so amusing as usual.

By the time he had smoked his after-dinner pipe he realized that very soon he would have to go to Margery Sinclair. "Wish I'd never promised Emily," he thought, eyeing the clock. "I've had a long day, and I may be up half the night if there's anything at the Perkinses' that that girl can't manage. I know what first confinements are by this time, if she doesn't. The Perkins woman has got no stamina. Very likely she'll give us a fright yet. I think I'll ring up Margery and say I can't come—she'd understand I could go and talk to her to-morrow morning—and stop by the fire now until I'm wanted."

He took a rueful glance at his bookshelves, felt the heat of the fire scorching his shins, and yielded for a moment to the exquisite drowsiness which dragged his head forward, and weighed down his eyelids and his hands, but a sharp recollection stabbed him awake and upright, as he found himself saying, "I promised Emily I'd save her telling the girl." He thought, "I'm funking that; Emily would see through me." And, staggering a little with sleep, he got up and went downstairs.

The cool air of the surgery revived him. The clock in the hall stood at five minutes to nine as he went out, unable to refrain from a glance at the empty, shining, mahogany surface of the table at the foot of the stairs. The post would be in at half-past nine; there might be two or three letters for him, or none, or simply the one alone; but for some reason he pictured it like that, menacing and solitary, awaiting him in the dark. The fancy followed him, and would not be shaken off, as he let himself out into the street and turned up toward the church. The night was cloudy and very dark; a light rain was beginning to fall and was whispering already about the roofs and corners of the houses; he saw it as a golden glitter beneath the infrequent lamps and turned up the collar of his old coat, for he hated rain as fastidiously as a cat does. He had not, however, far to go.

II

M A R G E R Y and her husband were established in a diminutive cottage at the corner of Water Lane and

Bridlesmith Gate. Doctor Serocold remembered it as having been occupied during his time in turn by a sweep, a policeman, and a pawnbroker, whose gilt balls had swung from what was now Margery's bedroom window; but that was before antiques and discomfort became the fashion. Margery had her mother's flair for a bargain. She had persuaded her husband to buy the tumbledown place for three hundred pounds from Jenkins the fishmonger, who was the ground landlord; and the young couple had spent most of their time during their short engagement in whitewashing, repapering, and repainting its six rooms. They had pickled a number of plastered and papered oak beams, found a blocked-up cupboard in the chimney stack, which Margery dignified by the name of the smugglers' hole, and uncovered a very satisfactory hearth with an inglenook, which a more provident tenant had bricked in to save firing. They raced about the country on the track of old furniture; and were in the habit of returning from sales with the back of their car disgracefully adorned by a rickety iron bedstead, a broken-legged table, or an assortment of kitchen china. Margery had always known what she wanted and how to get it: she was very much her mother's daughter in that. Doctor Serocold liked her little house and thought it characteristic of her. He always went there with pleasure; and he quickened his lagging and disheartened steps as he turned the corner of Bridlesmith Gate and saw her window throwing its wet glitter across the cobblestones.

The little cottage was called Gayfere's in old plans of the town. Its weather-tiled front was squeezed between two neighbours and looked as if it had become deformed by the pressure; it had a projecting upper story, a couple of lop-sided windows, one above the other, and a misshapen gable like the queen of spades' headdress in a pack of cards. There was an apology for a porch, not deep enough to afford any shelter, and supported by a couple of slender iron pillars painted white. Doctor Serocold stood outside the drip from this ridiculous adornment, of which his goddaughter was extremely proud, and looked in at her parlour window; but there seemed to be no one inside. The fire was burning brightly, however, and he could see cards and candles set out on the William and Mary walnut table, with its faded *petit-point* top, worked in a design of true-lovers'-knots and playing cards, which had been Margery's wedding present from her mother. Mrs. Unwin was a great needle-woman; and this particular piece of work had been her most successful restoration. Doctor Serocold, rattling at her daughter's knocker, remembered how she used to stitch away at it, and all her tricks of leaving it out in the sun, rubbing it with wet coffee grounds, and so forth. She had copied the design from a stained fragment which she had seen somewhere in a museum and had adapted it to the old table, declaring cheerfully that the finished piece would be worth anything she chose to ask from the London dealers. "I'm the best faker of embroidery in England." Doctor Serocold had never been quite sure whether she was or was not speaking seriously. However, she had handed over the table to Margery in the end, from one of her odd impulses of generosity. "Emily never could resist giving people what they wanted," thought Doctor Serocold, standing in the rain and wishing that Margery's maid would answer the door.

It was Margery herself, however, who eventually opened it, with a red-and-white pinafore over her black lace frock, her short brown curls in disorder, and a certain air of distraction unusual to her. "Hope you didn't knock twice," she said, pulling him in. "Jane's having her evening off . . . Baby's howling . . . Bill's gone down to the Highwayman to get some more whisky. He never told me we were short, curse him! And Mother's cried off coming, I can't think why. I've been ringing up the whole town to find a fourth for you."

She sounded annoyed, and Doctor Serocold, shaking himself out of his wet overcoat, remarked soothingly, "My dear, I don't care whether I get a game or not. I'd just as soon sit by your fire as my own." He hoped that she had not been successful in getting anyone. "For if she has," he reflected, "I'm done, and I might just as well have stayed at home. I can't talk to her about Emily with someone else there. Never thought of stopping her." He was annoyed with himself, and still more seriously annoyed when she remarked calmly. "Oh, you'll get your game all right. I told Kit Kennedy he'd have to put off whatever he was doing and come and help me out."

"The devil you did!" thought Doctor Serocold, who disliked the young man in question. "I wish I'd stayed at home."

A vexed silence was broken by the baby's wail from the bedroom upstairs. Doctor Serocold cocked an eyebrow and inquired, "What's the matter with Elspeth?"

"Nothing. She's just peevish," responded Margery with a frown which caused him to reflect, "Like her mother. . . ." He said aloud, "Shall I go up and have a look at her?"

"You can if you like," said Margery indifferently. "I shall have to go and stop that noise, anyhow." She went up before him two steps at a time, in one of her schoolgirl races. He followed more cautiously, being less familiar with her crooked and dangerous staircase, and found her standing defensively, with the child clutched in her arms. She faced him over its head as if she expected criticism. "There's nothing the matter with the kid," she declared crossly. "Just wants to be noticed."

He thought, "So do you, half the time," inconsequently, as he put an experienced finger on the baby's hot, damp, downy forehead. "You've been exciting her and yourself, I expect."

He drew his finger down the side of the child's face in an absent-minded caress before he asked, "Does she do much of this kind of thing?"

The crying had stopped; the child was only whimpering in a sleepy fashion, occasionally catching its breath. Margery stood rocking herself from one foot to the other and looking sulky. "Only does it when things are upset," she admitted. "Everything's been at sixes and sevens to-night. I can't help it. I've done my best. Bill's no help. He just says, 'Let things slide.'"

"And a very good motto, too," returned Doctor Serocold, watching her bright, flushed face and frowning forehead. "I thought I told you to settle down for six months and be a cow, Margery. You promised us you would."

"Well, it doesn't amuse me," burst out Margery. "I shall chuck it, and you can all say what you like. It's too dull. I didn't know what I was letting myself in for. Damn, there's the doorbell again."

She plumped the child down in its cot with more gentleness and skill than the doctor expected, whisked off the red-and-white pinafore, flung it across the bed with one swift, graceful movement, and was gone; he heard her running downstairs as lightly as she had come up. He remained a moment where he was, glancing round him and waiting to see if the child would wake again, but it did not stir. He had time to observe that the bedroom of the young couple had a little declined from its first precise elegance of chintz curtains, walnut furniture, patch-work and miniatures, to make room for a nursery litter of bottles and airing clothes. "I dare say the gilt *is* wearing off Margery's gingerbread a bit," he reflected, out of his experience, which had had its feminine aspects. "Ah, well, we've all got to grow up, worse luck!" He addressed the remark mentally to Elspeth in her pink muslin cot, but she made no further protest against life; and he went down the stairs with an older and heavier step than that of his goddaughter, thinking, "She'll only call it interfering if I give her any advice."

The two young men had either come back together, or else they had met on the doorstep. They were both in the parlour with Margery, who was giving all her attention to Kit Kennedy. He was a singularly handsome young fellow, fair-haired, well-made, and pleasant in his manners; his bleached eyebrows and moustache were almost white against his sunburned face. Doctor Serocold was obliged to admit that a girl must like to look at him. "It's the width between the eyes that's so attractive," he decided leisurely, finding himself left out of the conversation. "That and the shape of the mouth; both worth drawing. I expect she likes the way he smiles, too. Bill was always inclined to be sulky. Probably that interested her to begin with; she would fancy that she could tease him out of it, but she may be finding him heavier in hand that she thought." The big, dark, powerful young man was moving slowly about the room, fussing methodically

over his tray of drinks; Doctor Serocold suspected
that his wife found him a little irritating. "After
all, I often do myself, and I don't have to spend my
whole life with him. The other's got such a fascinating voice, too," he admitted, listening to it with
reluctant pleasure. "He could get round a little
goose like Margery any day he chose. Obviously
he's trying to. . . . I heard they'd been spending
a good deal of time together lately, since she got
about again. Of course in this place people gossip
if you speak to a woman twice; but I shouldn't be
surprised if there weren't something in it. Margery
was always a restless, changeable creature, and
to-night she's really being rather outrageous. Is she
showing off to Bill, or does she mean it? Kit Kennedy
always was a pretty good hand at a flirtation, and he
was certainly beginning to notice Margery the last
time he was home on leave. I had an idea she was
thinking about him, too, at that time. She was just
grown up and ready to fall in love with anyone.
Something might very well have come of it. But he
went back to the Sudan, to his cotton-growing, and
she started all that nonsense with her young flying
officer, and Bill got her in the end. I've always
thought it was partly because she was in the mood
and there was no one much else to think about.

This town is short of young men, like all country places nowadays. I dare say if she'd waited another year it might have been this young fellow instead. But when you get to my time of life you can't see why any one young couple should get married instead of another. The feeling's been growing on me lately. Margery and these two boys . . . Harry Catterick and Angela . . . my Scotch girl and her house surgeon . . . they all look alike to me . . . a lot of puppies or kittens with their eyes only just open . . . not yet able to tell good from bad. No wonder they make mistakes! I suppose we were just the same, but I can't realize it. After all, why did I marry Catherine, if it comes to that? She seemed to me different from all the others, but was she so different from all the others?"

He smiled sourly to himself, watching Bill Sinclair scowl at his wife as she lay sprawling half across her blue sofa with an engaging, boneless grace which fascinated the eye. "Bill ought to keep her in better order," he thought. "She looks about twelve years old with those long legs and that curly head. Absurd to think that she's the mother of that infant upstairs! She's going to be just as much of a handful as Emily was. Bill's too stupid to manage more than half of her. But then Tom could never handle even half of Emily; no more could I . . . no more could anyone. . . . That kind of woman always picks a man she can bewilder. Look what a fool her mother used to make of me! If Margery had been my daughter, though, I'd have brought her up to have better manners . . . lying there with her heels as high as her head, showing herself off to all of us. Not that she cares what Bill or I think of her; it's all for Kit tonight. I wonder how Bill's feeling?"

The young husband was sulking with his back to the fire, keeping it off everyone else in the room as he stroked the back of his head in an uncertain way that he had, and muttered, "If you want to play bridge, Margie, you'd better begin."

The doctor thought, "He hasn't a notion how to manage her. He lets her order him about too much nowadays . . . doesn't realize that it was a mistake to let her get the upper hand. That's just where Tom went wrong with Emily. He ought to have been master in his own house at Coldharbour. It wasn't fair that Emily should have had the burden of everything. But you couldn't argue with Emily. . . ." And he felt sorry for young Sinclair and annoyed with Margery, and said aloud. "Yes, you'd better get going. I might be sent for any time, and then where would you be?" It was more or less true, though he did not think that Jean Gordon would

send for him if she could help it. "She's too much
the other way inclined," he thought in passing.
"Likes to run her own shows. . . ."

Margery seemed impatient of the interruption and
grumbled. "Why don't you make your Scotch girl
do the night work? It's a shame people should come
bothering you when you've been at it all day." She
thumped the sofa cushion with her fist and pulled
it under her head with the gesture of a naughty
child refusing to move from a comfortable place. It
was young Kennedy who got to his feet politely,
breaking off the conversation and moving toward
the table, as the doctor remarked grimly, "I wish
a few more people in this town shared your views,
Margery. Eleven o'clock at night is the time I get
most of my calls. It's always the same story . . .
been feeling seedy all day and thought we'd just
send for you before we went to bed. It never occurs
to anyone that *I* may want to go to bed." They
were all three looking at Margery now, reluctantly
admiring her as she lay with her flushed, mischievous,
and smiling face obstinately pressed against the
cushion; until the doctor burst out with a flare of
impatience to the irresolute young man in front of
the fireplace, "Oh, for Heaven's sake, Bill, pull
her off that sofa, and let's get started."

Margery's eyes and mouth opened together in surprise, but she had no time to move before the command was obeyed. Doctor Serocold had spoken without any idea of so prompt a response, and certainly had not thought that young Sinclair would act so quickly. Margery was put on her feet with as much abrupt and undignified decision as if she had been a doll. She stood there blinking, ruffled and cross, without a word to say for herself. "Come, he's not such a fool as he looks," thought Doctor Serocold, oddly pleased, as Margery shook out her disordered lace skirts, tossed her hair away from her eyes, shrugged her sulky shoulders, and approached the card table with one foot childishly dragging past the other. Kit was shuffling the cards and looking for once a little silly. "He'd have liked to do it himself, but he wasn't quick enough," Doctor Serocold thought, with a flash of illumination. "Bill could cut him out all right if he chose. Perhaps the fellow understands his wife better than I do." And he pulled one of Margery's Hepplewhite chairs up to the table for himself.

III

T H E Y cut for partners, and he thought, as they began playing, "The Sinclair family against the world.
. . . Sounds all right, but they won't play as well together to-night as they usually do. Listen to Margery
now, bidding against her husband. That's her great
fault, she always wants to play the hand herself . . .
won't give in to her partner. . . . She's done it to me
before now and lost games by it. Bill always plays
a steady game, but he's backward with his calling.
My partner ought to be pleased with this." He
spread out his cards for young Kennedy and thought,
"Dummy sees most of the game. . . . Kit knows what
he's doing, all right; he won't make any mistake
with a hand like this. I hate that conceited way he
has, though, of pulling out the cards he thinks will be
wanted before he sees what the other side have really
led; I should change the lead just to spite him. But
perhaps that's what he aims for. Bad form, anyhow.
. . . I hate people to put down the honours half-way
through the hand. When I'm playing it confuses me
to be stopped. . . . I like this room of Margery's. The
child's made it very comfortable, as well as pretty;

she's got her mother's touch. I can't tell her about
Emily's business to-night; it'll have to stand over till
to-morrow. Let her have her evening to cheer her up,
and let her play the fool a bit if she likes. She's got
a hard time enough coming."

And he looked at her as she sat on his right, playing
out her cards with a little frown of concentration on
her forehead, and thought, "She's got eyes like
her mother, too . . . a couple of those little brown
specks in the gray of the iris . . . very fascinating
when you're close enough to notice them. I never
did till to-night." The last trick fell and he said,
"Thanks, partner: very satisfactory." Margery said,
rudely, "I don't see how you could help going game.
You had all the hearts in the pack. I do think Bill
might have raised me once more in my spades." Bill
retorted, with truth, "They had all the outsides.
They'd have gone on for ever"; and young Kennedy
calculated, "Forty and sixty-four . . . no, seventy-
two. Another hand like that would do us nicely,
sir." Doctor Serocold grunted, "I dare say. . . ."

The game went on for a couple of hours, with
varying fortunes. Margery played badly and held
poor cards; her husband played carefully and came
out even; the doctor won something, and Kennedy
a good deal more: Margery paid the table. She was

a controlled but not a cheerful loser: she became more and more gloomy as the evening went on, and paid, the doctor thought, less and less attention to her cards. Kit condoled with her on her bad luck, and her husband pointed out some of her more obvious errors. She was equally short with both of them. At eleven, or a little before it, when it appeared that her luck was out for the night, Doctor Serocold refused to begin another rubber. "I've got to look in on a case on my way home," he declared, not quite truthfully, as Bill protested that it was still early. "And I didn't really want to play to-night at all. I was up till three this morning. I could do with a little sleep."

Kit said something pleasant, and Bill something sympathetic: Margery sat with her arms folded among the scattered cards on the table and did not press the doctor to stay. "Don't keep the poor man out of his bed," she protested ungraciously to her husband. "Last rubbers are always long ones: everybody overbids. We've had enough of that to-night as it is. Do let him clear out if he wants to. You always try to go on till next day. I'm yawning my head off." She was so like a disappointed child at the end of a dull party that even her husband was amused by her inhospitality.

"Oh, pack her off upstairs, Bill," said the doctor. "She's half asleep."

"Yes, you clear off, Margie," her husband said, kindly enough. He was standing just behind her, and he put his arm round her shoulders and pulled her to her feet. Doctor Serocold expected her to resist, and for a moment she seemed inclined to do so: but then she yielded, leaned back against her husband, and shut her eyes and opened her mouth in an exhausted yawn. "Don' wanna' stay up," she murmured in a drowsy fashion. She appeared to have lost all interest in the three men who stood looking at her. She gave young Kennedy the same limp hand that she gave to Doctor Serocold, and went off as meekly as a child that has been sent to bed. The doctor thought, "Perhaps he can manage her after all."

If young Kennedy had wanted to linger, he got no chance; Bill said firmly that he would see the two of them home. They stepped out into a street where the rain had ceased to fall, and the air smelt fresh; the wet cobblestones reflected the gleam of an infrequent lamp. They left Kit at his father's house, at the corner of Whitsun Street, and the doctor half expected Bill to turn back when that had been accomplished; but he lingered under a street lamp with the same vague indecision which he had shown on his own hearth, inquiring, "Where are you off to, Doctor?"

"Depends," said Doctor Serocold. "Miss Gordon went out to a case in Station Road. I'll just go back to the surgery and find out if there's been any message. She may be home by this time; and if she is, she'll have written me a note and left it as she went by. Then I can turn in. If she hasn't done that, and if I'm not wanted elsewhere, I may just step down and see what she's up to."

He yawned, and Bill said, "Thought you were goin' to bed." He sounded amused, and the doctor laughed as he admitted, "Well, I am . . . some time." They went down the steep street in an amiable silence; but when they reached the corner of the High Street the doctor said, "If you come any farther with me you'll find Margery asleep by the time you get back."

They were about to cross the road, and Bill's immediate reply was, "Here, look out for that puddle." He took the older man by the arm as they stepped across a pool of black rainwater standing above a blocked gutter. It was not until they had made their way across the uneven cobblestones of the hill, and he had muttered, "The town council ought to put more lamps in these streets at night,"

that Bill said, "She seems a bit overdone . . . think
I'll sleep on the sofa."

"Shouldn't do that if I were you," muttered
Doctor Serocold, and they walked some way in
silence between the shuttered shop-fronts of the
High Street before he added, cautiously, "Takes a
bit of managing, doesn't she?"

"You bet she does," agreed Bill gloomily.

"Think you give her too much rope?" Doctor
Serocold glanced sideways to find out whether this
would offend the young husband; but the road was
too dark for him to judge. The voice that replied to
him sounded merely tired. "I've tried all ways. I
don't like to lose my temper too often. She's such
a kid."

"Nice to watch," hazarded the doctor, and got a
sort of protesting groan for answer.

"I suppose he can't be too hard on anything so
pretty, at his age," he thought; and said aloud,
"Take it easy. She's not done so badly, considering
how young she was when you got hold of her."
"Won't be twenty-one till December," agreed Bill,
and found nothing to add to it. The doctor's red
lamp appeared in the distance before he betrayed
his thoughts by saying, without apparent reason,
"Kennedy's leave will be up next month."

The doctor thought it best to overlook that damaging admission of anxiety. "He'd rather persuade himself to-morrow that I didn't notice it," he decided; and said, "Perhaps I'm inclined to spoil Margery. But then I've known her ever since she was born."

"Well, if it comes to that, so have I," said Margery's husband, and the doctor heard him laugh for the first time that evening. Encouraged by this, he stopped at his own door and said earnestly, "Look here, my boy, I haven't any business to tell you this yet, but you'll have to know sooner or later. There's bad news for Margery. Keep it to yourself to-night. Her mother's seriously ill . . . there'll have to be an operation. I saw her to-day, but I couldn't tell Margery, with that young fool there." Somehow the epithet relieved his feelings. He could not go on for the moment; his recollection of Emily Unwin was too clear. He was only partly conscious of the young man's shocked inquiries and his own explanations: he had been through such scenes too often not to foresee everything that would need to be said and done, and for once he cut the business short. He was suddenly too tired to talk any longer. "I'll go over it all with you to-morrow," he said wearily. "Let Margery have her night's rest, though. She's got a bad time coming. She and her mother are devoted to each other. You'll have to see her through."

He felt that Emily had made no mistake, as he saw the young man steady his shoulders to receive this burden. "Emily said I could leave Margery to him," he remembered. "She was right: there's more in him than one thinks." And he said goodnight to young Sinclair with more affection than was usual between them. "A good boy . . ." he thought, watching the tall figure receding down the street.

He entered his own narrow house and passed through the dim, empty waiting room to the foot of the stairs. The gas was turned down to a pin-point above the mahogany table: but he made out, with a shock of recollection, that there were three letters upon it. The slate with its string and attached pencil lay beside them; there was some message upon its surface, but he could not see to read either that or the addresses upon the letters, and for the moment he was incapable of the simple action of reaching up his hand to the light. He performed it after a hesitation of which he was ashamed, and some incalculable perversity made him look first at the slate. Jean Gordon had written on it, as she always did, the address to which she had gone and her time of departure, eight-thirty: if she had returned she would have scratched it out.

"I shall have to go down there, then," he said to himself mechanically, as he turned to the letters.

They were all three for him. The first was an advertisement of some patent medicine, with the name of an American firm stamped upon it; the second was a private letter, with the local postmark; the third was what he expected. He turned it over with an unsteady hand, unconsciously noting the weight of the packet, the typed address and the printed name of his hospital on the face of the large envelope, the crest on its flap, a laurel branch entwined with the Æsculapian snake, and the Latin motto familiar to him from his student days. His fingers told him. "There's the gastric analysis in this, and a letter from Phillips, and probably the X-ray photographs: I shall know what's the matter with me inside five minutes."

He found that he could not stand on his feet any longer; he sat down in the chair beside the table, where his waiting patients sat, rested the hand with the letter in it on his knee, and thought, "I must have a minute to get used to this," and with complete inconsequence he said to himself, in another part of his mind, "The light's bad here, or else it's my eyes. I must get Purvis to put in a new mantle to-morrow. He's always slack about those little things." He tried to swallow with his dry lips and could not do it: he had a sick, empty feeling under his ribs, where the pain had been, the blood was ringing in his ears. He shut his eyes for a moment and screwed up his eyelids; when he opened them again he was dazed, and could see nothing for a moment. Then he perceived the letter in his hand and opened it.

The first thing that came to his hand was the typed report of his test meal, from the clinical laboratory, a couple of sentences lost in the middle of a page. He read them without difficulty, holding the paper at full stretch of his arm to accommodate his lengthening sight: but, straightforward as they were, they seemed to have no meaning for him. He said to himself, bewildered, "But that can't be *my* report. There's nothing wrong with it . . . practically normal, as far as the acidity goes. Have they made a mistake . . . sent me someone else's? No, there's my name on it. What's Phillips's report? Nobody trusts these laboratory findings nowadays . . . got to get them clinically confirmed." He found that he had dropped the report, and with it a couple of blurred photographs and a letter. He groped for them between his feet, grunting heavily, as he always did nowadays when he had to stoop, and flushing up to his forehead with vexation. The papers were difficult to get up from the floor: he scraped at their edges with his fingers and crumpled them together in his hands. The photographs appeared normal: he stared at their blurred shadows, and found nothing unusual in them; but it seemed to him that he had forgotten what to look for. A layman could not have been more bewildered. He turned in despair to the letter itself: he could no longer trust his own eyes or mind.

The specialist had written a couple of pages, in a vile handwriting; he made out a sentence here and there. "Glad to send you such satisfactory information . . . took a more formidable . . . no, favourable . . . view from the first than you did yourself . . . nervous dyspepsia aggravated by"—could the word be *overwork?* " . . . Think you need have no further . . ."—he did make out the word—"anxiety. . . . Three months' treatment, as I recommended." He said aloud, "Why can't the old fool use a typewriter?" He did not go on to the second page, which appeared to be directions as to his diet, but stuffed the whole bundle of papers back together into the big envelope, pushed it across the table beside him, and put up both hands to his forehead. It was as wet as if he had been running in a race, and he said to himself, with a short, desperate, exhausted laugh, "I'm getting too old for this sort of thing."

The papers lay where he had put them and he glanced at them sideways as if they were still dangerous. "My God, what a shock!" he thought confusedly. "Somehow, I'd made up my mind the other way. All day . . . all these days . . . I've been getting more and more certain that I was done for. Queer, the way one's mind works. . . . I'm frightfully upset by this. I could have stood bad news better. I was ready for that. I feel as if the ground had been cut away under my feet . . . as if I were on the scaffold, and they'd just worked the drop. It's the other way about, though. . . . I'm reprieved, and I don't know what to do about it. I feel . . . I feel like a fool."

He began to laugh again, but this time it was with a long, strange, uncertain sound. "I shall have to pull myself together," he thought incoherently, "get something to do. Good thing there was no one here to see me!" He found that his unsteady fingers had taken up and unfolded the American advertisement. Its enthusiastic periods conveyed no meaning to him whatever. "Doctor, are your patients satisfied with your diagnosis?" he read bemusedly; and again, lower down, "Doctor, are *you* satisfied with your diagnosis?" He turned the thing over in a vain effort to find out what it was all about, and then suddenly the words themselves acquired an independent significance. Something seemed to break in him, and he gave a cackle of relief. "I suppose I ought to be," he admitted, with a grin; and he crumpled up the mysteriously appropriate appeal in a hand which had regained its usual vigour.

He examined his third letter mechanically: it was only old Miss Wright, at Holt Abbas, asking him to come over some day and see her about her eyes. "I could have done that to-day, if I'd known," he thought. "I must have been right past her door, about a quarter to seven." And then he thought fantastically, "But that was a hundred years ago. . . ."

He raised his fatigued eyes to the grandfather clock at the foot of the stairs and forced his mind to consider the hour. It was twenty-five minutes to twelve. "Almost to-morrow morning," he calculated. He felt light and empty, and a little cold; he thought, "It's been a heavy day . . . one of the worst. This hanging over me all the time . . . I've hardly known what I was doing. Well, it's all over now." And he thought, "I suppose I shall take it in some time. Just at present I don't seem able to make any plans. This alters everything. I shall have to make up my mind what to do about the partnership . . . and that girl . . . and everything. I can't face it all. I'm too tired and too discouraged. If it weren't so fantastic, I should say that I'm disappointed." And he remembered Emily Unwin.

"She's saved herself the trouble of beginning again," he realized. "I believe now I understand her."

His head dropped on his breast, and a soft stupor overcame him. He longed to sleep where he was, and to sleep for ever. For a moment he did actually lose consciousness; his breathing steadied and deepened, his lips fell apart, and the air began to puff and whistle faintly as it escaped between them. The sound of it awakened him again with a guilty start. He stared about him as he tried to recollect where he was and what he had to do; then got heavily to his feet, reminding himself that he had work to finish.

"That girl's still out at her case," he remembered. "I shall have to go along and see what's happening. I wish those damned Perkinses were on the telephone! She'd send for me if she wanted me, and if she had anyone to send: but I'd rather go out now than get to bed and then turn out again. . . . Queer, how one never really gets used to nightwork. I suppose I shall have to go on with it now till further notice. Of course, I could still retire in a few months, when things have straightened themselves out . . . settle down somewhere near here, in the country, and get a bit of fishing and enjoy myself, instead of working myself to death." But somehow the prospect did not really attract him. He had ceased to consider it by the time that he had crammed his letters into his bulging breast pocket, made his way, more by habit than by his sense of sight, into the dimly lighted surgery, and lugged out the second and larger of the two midwifery bags from the bottom of the cupboard, where he kept them.

"She's got the chloroform down there already," his dazed and drowsy mind was able to calculate. "But probably by this time we shall need the other things. Better take 'em on the chance and save coming back. It's only seven minutes' walk: I can't be bothered to shift the car out of the garage. I'll just go down on foot and get the job over; and then I can go to bed."

IV

H E L E T himself out of the front door quietly, descended the High Street, and turned along Friar Lane; as he passed between the twin towers of the Barbican gate he heard three-quarters strike, and

realized that a new day would soon begin. He
yawned and shivered and thought, "Forty years of
this sort of thing is no joke. A doctor's life is a dog's
life. I didn't know what I was letting myself in for
when I took it on. If I had my time over again I'd
choose some job where I could have my nights in
bed."

He changed the heavy bag from one hand to the
other, resting it on his bent knee for a moment;
closed and unclosed his stiffened, burning fingers,
and beat them once or twice against his thigh to set
the blood flowing through them. The raw damp of
the October night showed him his own breath hanging about him in a cloud as he paused under a lamp;
the sweat was hot on his forehead and sticky between
his shoulders, and he said to himself irritably, "I
was a fool to come out again with this ton weight of
stuff. I wish I'd left the girl to get on by herself. Ten
to one when I get there she won't need me, and it'll
all be over." The nagging, sour pain had begun again
under his ribs, and he repeated to himself, "Nervous
dyspepsia, aggravated by overwork. Serves me right
for hurrying along with this dead weight. I can't go
on doing everything I used to do. I've got to try and
remember that I'm sixty-five. This is the way my
elderly patients kill themselves." He mopped his

forehead and calculated, "The house can't be much farther, anyhow. Fifteen, Station Road." He set out again, trying to make himself go slower, changing the bag from hand to hand at increasingly short intervals, and anxiously counting the street lamps in their wet haloes ahead of him until he reached the corner and saw the red lights at the level crossing shining like quiet jewels across his path. "Just my luck," thought he. "The eleven-fifty. Well, she'll be through before I get there." For he was one of those people who cherish a quiet passion for railway time-tables and trains.

The rails were humming already as he put down his heavy bag in the road beside the level crossing and rested his hands on the topmost bar of the small swing gate. The humming grew to a steady beat, to a roar and a rattle, to a storm of noise that deafened him, and a rush of air that blinded him. The express went by within six feet of him, and left him clinging to the gate; by the time that he had his breath again the signals had changed to green, and a few loose pieces of paper were fluttering and settling along the line. He thought obscurely, "Not much left if that hit you. Never know anything about it. I like trains . . ." and then, "Got to get on with my job, too, I suppose."

The long gates across the road clanked, shifted and began to open; he pushed through the small gate and stumbled across the still vibrating rails, crunching the ballast underfoot between them.

The house he had to visit was not more than a hundred yards farther, one of a row of cheap, jerry-built villas, in dark-red brick, with slated roofs and dwarf bow windows; a street lamp revealed the clipped privet hedge behind the scrolled ironwork and low wall that divided its garden from the road. Doctor Serocold knew the bedrooms of the whole row from One to Twenty: they did not differ from each other in any material particular. He saw the light burning between the slats of the Venetian blinds on the first floor of Number Fifteen, and said to himself, "Still at it."

The man who answered his ring was yawning, unshaven and haggard. He muttered, "No luck yet, sir," and stood aside to let him in. The doctor shed his heavy overcoat, took up the bag again, and mounted the stairs in his own quiet and deliberate manner. The door of the front bedroom was ajar; he pushed it open and went in.

The room was hot, brightly lit, and crowded with furniture. He had to make his way carefully between the marble-topped washstand and the foot of the big double bed; and even so his elbow knocked off one of the loose brass knobs from the iron frame and sent it rattling along the floor. He kicked irritably at some unseen obstacle underfoot, which felt like a doubled and displaced strip of Japanese matting; avoided the bellying white lace curtain which strained at its blue-ribbon sash in the wind blowing through the drawn Venetian blinds; and set down the black bag with a grunt of relief on a black sheepskin rug, between a red velvet, anti-macassared armchair and a rickety bamboo table, from which a couple of flowering geraniums had not yet been displaced. Then he looked round to get his bearings.

Jean Gordon was standing on the other side of the room, with her back to a roasting little fire, her sleeves up to her elbows, and a ginger-coloured mackintosh apron covering her from neck to knees.

She just nodded to him, and then her watchful eyes went back to the woman in the bed; she looked rosy, hot, and serious, but not alarmed; he recognized her professional air. A little old woman beside her, in a decent black frock and apron, he placed as the patient's mother, come to stay for the occasion. She was a stranger to him: Perkins, the station master, had married a London girl. The woman fixed her bright, frightened eyes upon the new doctor and

sucked her false teeth nervously, but did not speak;
she took up one corner of her apron and twisted it
restlessly in her hands. He looked finally at the patient herself, and found her flushed, drowsy, and
groaning, with her face half-buried in the pillow, and
a corner of it between her teeth. She appeared unconscious of his arrival, even when he put his fingers
on the moist wrist of the hand that clutched at the
blanket, and felt for the thin hurry of her pulse.
Jean stepped up to the other side of the bed· and to
her he said, scarcely moving his lips, "Well, what
about it?"

She replied, in an undertone that matched his, "I
was thinking of sending the husband up for you.
Everything's quite straightforward, but very slow,
and she's getting tired out. I thought we might . . ."
She did not finish her sentence, but glanced first
at the old woman watching them with her bright,
anxious eyes, and then at the bag he had brought
with him. He nodded thoughtfully and kept his fingers on the woman's wrist for another half-minute;
then sighed, turned away from the bed and said,
"Well, let's get some of these cursed plants out of
the way and shift the bed a foot or two from the
wall. Is that kettle boiling? Good. Then clear out
downstairs, Mrs. Whatever-your-name-is, and bring

up a fresh lot of hot water when we shout for it;
and stop in the kitchen till we do. And tell Perkins
we shan't be much longer." And when the door had
shut behind her he said to the Scotch girl, "You
can get on with this if you like, Child. It's your
show."

And a little later, sitting sideways behind the pillow, and squeezing the rubber bulb of the chloroform
inhaler between his fingers, he thought, "Feather
bed, as usual, and the gas on, and the room like an
oven with that fire burning. How do the women stand
it? Nice atmosphere to work in! Well, the girl's got
the worst end of it. I can see the damp on her forehead. But it wouldn't have been fair to do her out of
her bit of fun. After all, it's her case, and she's new
to things. When she's been through this business as
often as I have she won't find it quite so thrilling.
I must say she knows her job, and she's very neat
with her fingers. She's doing this quite prettily and
carefully, no clumsy hurry. . . . Cool as a cucumber
. . . sort of thing I like to watch. Got one trick when
she's absorbed, though: she sticks her tongue out of
the corner of her mouth, like a kitten. I shall tease
her about that some day when I know her better. . . .
Yes, I'm beginning to feel as if I could make plans
again one of these days, when I'm rested. And she'll

be in them, with that young man of hers, if he suits. I've got to add up my own sums, and make room for the younger generation, and I may as well do it gracefully . . . get my fun out of it and earn a little gratitude."

The fumes from the anæsthetic were beginning to make him a little drowsy and confused. He thought, "I've seen four generations to-day, wandering round, seen the whole of my own life again, in a way, and had a chance to tell what it's been worth. Gaunt was one of a lot that were here before me and are dropping off now like falling leaves, one after the other. My own generation is running dry . . . all the old shopkeepers that I've watched building up their businesses . . . the General, and Martha Purefoy, and poor silly old Jamieson . . . all that crowd fussing about at the council, and that devilish old hag out at Carfax, and my poor Emily and myself. We've had our chances and done what we could with them . . . good or bad, there's not much more to be expected of us. . . . And the generation in between are dead and buried, like Gaunt's sons and Jimmy Canfield, or spoiled and smashed and left on the rubbish heap like Harry Catterick, and Ellen Archibald, and Meek. . . . But there's a new lot coming up to take our places, and not such a bad lot, either. I've no child of my own to leave behind me . . . wish I had. . . . But Mary Gaunt and that young couple at the vicarage would sell their souls to bring their children up properly, and Emily's daughters are going to make good wives and mothers in the end, and Harry's Angela will pull him out of the fire; even that little slut of Martha's will probably produce a child worth having. And this girl and her husband will take over my job when I'm gone to Catherine, and make a better thing of it than I did, I shouldn't wonder."

He found himself nodding over the bottle under his nose, pulled himself up with a start and realized suddenly, "Here comes the last of the procession. Lively little beggar, in spite of everything . . . worth stopping up after midnight for, I suppose. Anyhow, his mother'll think him worth the trouble, when she comes round."

He got off the bed and came to watch the mother, while Jean Gordon took the child. "Not a bad specimen, that," he observed. "Ought to turn the scale at seven, I should say. But there's not much doubt about our simian ancestry, is there? They're all exactly like chimpanzees at this stage. Look at those feet! He could put the soles of them flat against each other, they're so turned in. And he'll hang on to one of your fingers as if he still lived in the branches."

Jean had the squirming, greasy, plump creature
in her arms, and was carrying it round to the fire.
She laughed, but did not reply. He observed her
maternal attitude as she seated herself by the waiting
cradle and began wrapping the child in an old blanket
on her knees. She was for the moment entirely absorbed and unconscious, and he thought, "Yes, she'll
look like that some day with her own." Then he had
to turn his attention to the woman under his hand,
who was beginning to murmur and stir. . . .

Half an hour later Jean had cleared up the mess,
and he and she were stepping out together into the
wet fog. As the rusty gate creaked behind them and
they turned back to the town together, she said in
her youthful, confident voice, "Now, that's the sort
of case I like. One feels one's been of some use."

He nodded thoughtfully, strolling beside her, and
agreed, "Yes, it's about the most satisfying thing
we do. There's a certain incurable hopefulness about
it . . . one imagines the creature may be going to
have a better chance than one did oneself. If only
they wouldn't keep one out of bed till such uncon-
scionable hours. . . ."

They had reached the signal box, and the light
from it fell on his upturned face; he put his hand
on the gate of the level crossing to open it for the

girl, and she saw that he was smiling. She said remorsefully, "You've had a long day."

"Not too bad," said he. "Pretty typical. But it's seemed to me like a long one. I'm glad it's over. . . ." And he said to himself, more than to her, "I ought to sleep like a log to-night."

The day that had begun with an old man's death had ended with the birth of a child.

THE END